# Tweenie Genie

# Tweenie Genie

## Genie in Training

### Meredith Badger

FEIWEL AND FRIENDS

NEW YORK

A FEIWEL AND FRIENDS BOOK
An imprint of Macmillan

TWEENIE GENIE: GENIE IN TRAINING. Text copyright © 2009 by Meredith Badger. Illustration and design copyright © 2009 by Hardie Grant Egmont. All rights reserved. Printed in December 2010 in the United States of America by R. R. Donnelley & Sons Company, Crawfordsville, Indiana. For information, address Feiwel and Friends, 175 Fifth Avenue, New York, N.Y. 10010.

A CIP catalogue record for this book is
available from the National Library of Australia

ISBN: 978-0-312-65782-6

Originally published in Australia by Hardie Grant Egmont

Feiwel and Friends logo designed by Filomena Tuosto

Cover and text design by Sonia Dixon Design
Illustrations by Michelle Mackintosh

First published in the United States by Feiwel and Friends,
an imprint of Macmillan

First U.S. Edition: 2011

10 9 8 7 6 5 4 3 2 1

www.feiwelandfriends.com

# Chapter 1

You probably know someone who is like Poppy Miller. Like how she used to be, that is.

You know those kinds of people who stand out in a crowd? Who everyone turns to stare at, for no particular reason, when they walk down the street? Those types who always know the right answer to everything their teacher asks them, even if they don't seem to be paying attention? The ones who come in first at every sport they play, even if they're not really trying?

Well, Poppy Miller was *nothing* like that.

Not that there was anything wrong with her. Far from it. She had a pleasant face, and long, straight brown hair that she wore in a ponytail, just like lots of girls her age.

She definitely wasn't tall, but she wasn't the shortest girl in class, either. She wasn't the top student, but she also wasn't the worst one. She wasn't bad at sports, but she never seemed to win ribbons or trophies.

Do you see what we're getting at? Poppy Miller was like lots of other girls her age. Normal. Average. *Ordinary*.

But then, on the evening of her twelfth birthday, Poppy found something that changed her life forever. Totally, utterly, and completely. Something so incredible that nothing would ever be the same again. It was a . . .

But hang on, we're getting ahead of ourselves. To understand properly just how amazing this thing was, we need to go back. Back to the start of the party.

**Sunday, October 17th, 3:05pm**

The moment Poppy walked into the living room where her twelfth birthday party was being held, she knew she'd been totally wrong about the event. It wasn't going to be terrible, embarrassing, and painfully awkward at all. Oh, no.

It was going to be the *most* terrible, *most* embarrassing, *most* awkward event in the history of terrible, embarrassing, and awkward events. And if you think Poppy was over-reacting, let's look at the facts.

First, Poppy's mom had insisted on having a ladybug theme, so the whole room—in fact, the whole house—was decorated with spotty little red bugs. Poppy's dad was passing around ladybug cupcakes while wearing ladybug feelers on his head. It looked like a party for someone turning three years old, not *twelve*.

To make things worse, there wasn't a single person in the room who Poppy considered to be her friend.

Plus, she was wearing jeans and her favorite bright red top, which was nice, but not exactly party material. The final straw was when Poppy looked down at her feet and realized she still had her slippers on. Her *bunny* slippers.

*OK, time to go and find a place to hide*, Poppy

decided. But before she could escape from the living room, Poppy's mom put a firm hand on her shoulder.

"Look, everyone!" she announced, cheerfully. "It's our big birthday girl!"

Everyone in the room turned and stared. Instantly, Poppy felt her face flush with embarrassment. *Great*, she thought. *Now, I look like a tomato. A tomato wearing bunny slippers.*

You have to admit, it wasn't a great start to being twelve years old.

Poppy had tried very hard to talk her mom out of throwing this party.

"Twelve is such a nothing-y age," Poppy explained. She meant it, too. Being twelve meant you weren't a little kid anymore, but

5

you weren't a teenager yet, either. You were stuck somewhere in between. Everyone knew being twelve was bad. Everyone, it seemed, except Poppy's mother.

"It's not a nothing-y age!" she cried indignantly. "You're a *tweenager*. That's a terrific thing to be, darling. We threw a wonderful teddy bear party when your sister turned twelve. Astrid said it was her favorite party ever."

*Of course she did*, thought Poppy darkly.

Poppy couldn't have been more different than her sister, Astrid, if she'd tried. She was different from her whole family, really. Poppy *looked* completely different, for one thing. Her parents and her sister were all fair and athletic. Poppy was dark and—well, let's be honest here—she was kind of short and skinny.

But the differences weren't just on the

outside. Poppy's parents and sister thought the perfect day was one spent hiking, or doing a fifteen-mile bike ride together. Or hiking and *then* bike riding. Poppy much preferred to spend the day in one of her favorite hiding spots, reading, listening to music, or just daydreaming.

The mantelpiece in the Millers's den was covered with trophies and certificates, and not just for sporting events, either. Astrid had won awards for math and spelling competitions. Poppy's mom had won a trophy for being on a game show. And Poppy's dad had even won a trophy for inventing a brand-new style of trophy.

Visitors to the Millers's house always exclaimed, "What an extraordinary family you are!"

But none of the prizes belonged to Poppy because there were only two things that she was good at. One was touching her nose with her tongue. The other was squeezing into tiny hiding places. She'd been doing these things since she was a baby, and the family photo album was full of pictures of the different boxes and cupboards Poppy had squeezed into over the years. But, of course, no one gave out prizes for those kinds of skills.

*I MUST be adopted*, Poppy told herself a thousand times a day. *It's the only way to explain how different I am!*

After all, if Poppy's mom really was her mom, she would have guessed the other huge reason why Poppy didn't want to have a party this year. It was because there was no one she wanted to invite. Absolutely no one.

ordinary hair and ordinary eyes

never cries

likes: pink yogurt, cheese curls, reading, dancing, writing in her diary

note: no big secrets AT ALL!

has her own style

dislikes: hiking, people who snoop, fashion clones

Poppy

Current favorite hiding spot: cupboard under the stairs

"Go and chat with Claudette and your other little friends while I get the cake," Poppy's mom instructed, pushing her toward a group of smirking girls.

Poppy groaned inwardly. She and Claudette had been really good friends in elementary school. But since they'd started middle school this year, it felt like they had nothing in common anymore. All Claudette talked about these days was fashion and the school magazine she'd started called *School Style*. She and her new friends all wore identical outfits and hairdos. Worst of all, they were always hassling Poppy to let them give her makeovers.

Poppy secretly called them the Clothes Club, and if she'd been given a choice between being thrown into a cage of hungry lions or talking to the Clothes Club girls, Poppy would've said, "Where's that cage?"

But Poppy hadn't been given a choice, so she reluctantly walked over. The Clothes Club girls were all wearing striped black and hot pink dresses over black leggings. And they all had their hair pinned back with matching sparkly clips.

"Hi, guys," said Poppy, trying her best to smile. "Thanks for coming. Can I offer you a ladybug crunch? Or spotted JELL-O, perhaps?"

Claudette didn't seem to hear. She was too busy looking at Poppy's clothes. "What on *earth* are you wearing, Poppy?" she said, sounding horrified.

The other girls giggled.

"You could be so cute if you tried," Claudette

added. "Maybe even cute enough to be in *School Style*—but then you go and wear things like those." She pointed at Poppy's feet.

Oh, yeah. The bunny slippers.

Right then, Poppy knew she had a choice. She could curl up and die of shame. Or she could pretend she'd worn the slippers on purpose. So Poppy smiled proudly and stuck out her foot. "Aren't they *divine*?" she said. "They're from Paris, you know."

"As if!" Claudette snorted. "Now, why don't you let me give you a makeover? It can be part of my present to you."

"Ummm," said Poppy, backing away. "Well, I—ahh . . ."

Then she walked straight into someone. It was her big sister, Astrid. Recently, Astrid had started insisting that Poppy must have a really special talent for *something*—especially in a family where everyone else was so exceptional.

"Happy birthday, sis!" said Astrid. "Now that you're twelve, I'm *sure* we'll find something about you that's, you know, really *special*."

Poppy sighed. *Not this again!* Most of the time Poppy just ignored it when Astrid talked like this. But sometimes, it really got to her. And right now was one of those times.

"Listen carefully, Astrid," Poppy said as calmly as she could. "I really *am* this ordinary. I'm a normal, average girl. No incredible talents, no surprises up my sleeve. Got it?"

"Oh, don't talk like that," tutted Astrid, patting Poppy on the shoulder. "I'm sure there's *something* you're good at!"

Just then, the lights dimmed and Poppy's

mom appeared carrying an enormous red-and-black cake. No prizes for guessing what it was shaped like.

"Blow out the candles and make a wish!" said Poppy's mom, after everyone had sung "Happy Birthday."

Poppy looked down at the cake. This was it. The moment she'd been dreading. The point at which she officially became a tweenager.

*What should I wish for?* wondered Poppy. There were so many things she wanted to change right now. Too many things to sum up in one little wish. So Poppy just made the best wish she could think of: *I wish EVERYTHING were different*.

Poppy didn't really believe in wishes, but she still couldn't help glancing around hopefully after the wish had been made.

Nothing had changed. Not one thing.

*And nothing ever will*, thought Poppy gloomily.

When the party had finally finished, Poppy gratefully escaped to her room. The rest of her family were in the kitchen having a cleanup competition, but as the birthday girl, Poppy had been excused. She leaned against her bedroom door, relieved that the day was over.

It was then that she noticed it. The thing that was to change her life forever.

Sitting on her bedside table was a strange-looking bottle, bright and glimmeringly green with a long, smooth neck.

# Chapter 2

Poppy looked at the bottle curiously. It definitely hadn't been there that morning.

She walked over and picked it up. It was heavy in her hands, but surprisingly warm. Was there something inside it? Poppy pulled out the stopper and peered in. It seemed empty, but there was the faint smell of something good that Poppy couldn't quite put her finger on. Was it apple pie, maybe? Or cinnamon donuts?

*It must be a birthday present,* decided Poppy. But from whom? Her family had already given her their gifts (some hiking boots and a bike tire repair kit, which Poppy had immediately stashed at the back of her closet). Poppy looked around for a card, but there wasn't one. It was all very weird.

She held the bottle up to the light, admiring the way it sparkled and glowed. *Well, the person who gave it to me obviously has good taste,* she decided. *But they could've given it a scrub first!* The bottle was dusty, if not downright dirty.

Poppy gave the bottle a quick rub with a hanky. And then something strange happened. First, the spicy, apple-y smell grew very strong. Then thick, purplish smoke began pouring out of the bottle. Alarmed, Poppy dropped it. The bottle rolled, but didn't break, and smoke kept pouring out until the entire room was purple.

Poppy was about to start yelling "Fire!" when there was a loud *POP!* and the smoke suddenly stopped.

Then Poppy heard coughing. She froze. There was someone else in the room!

"Astrid, if that's you playing a trick, you're really not funny," Poppy said, trying to sound tougher than she felt. Astrid was always snooping around Poppy's room.

Then someone spoke. "That bottle needs a tune-up," a girl said, wildly waving her hands around. "It shouldn't smoke this much."

Poppy's heart beat even faster. It definitely wasn't Astrid. So who was it?

When the smoke finally cleared, Poppy found herself face-to-face with a teenage girl

who had startlingly green eyes and extremely long, dark hair pulled up into a very high ponytail. She reminded Poppy of one of the cool, older girls at her middle school—the ones that always totally ignored the younger kids.

She was wearing the strangest outfit Poppy had ever seen. Her puffy skirt sat low on her hips and her top was made from fabric so soft and light that it seemed to float around her. The outfit should have looked dumb. But it didn't. It looked incredible!

Which was why, just for a moment, Poppy found herself behaving more like the Clothes Club girls than like herself.

"Where did you get your clothes?" she asked curiously.

"That's not important right now," replied the girl briskly. "I've got things to tell you and

I need you to pay attention."

"Hang on a minute!" said Poppy, putting her hands on her hips. She hated being bossed around. "Who *are* you? And what are you doing in my room?"

"I would've thought that was pretty obvious," replied the girl, "seeing as I've just popped out of a bottle. I'm a genie."

You've probably worked out that Poppy was a logical girl. She'd never been into fairies. She was skeptical about ghosts. And she'd never even *considered* believing in genies. But that was before one had appeared in front of her.

"If you're a genie," Poppy said, thinking fast, "doesn't that mean you have to grant me three wishes?"

The genie sighed, like she was dealing with a very small child. "No, it doesn't mean that at all."

"Why not?" asked Poppy.

"Because genies can't grant wishes for other genies." The girl shrugged, like it was common knowledge.

"What other genie?" said Poppy, puzzled.

The genie rolled her eyes. "YOU, of course!"

That was when Poppy started laughing. She laughed so hard that she had to sit down. This girl was clearly nuts!

"Are you quite finished?" asked the girl eventually.

"I'm sorry," said Poppy, wiping her eyes. "But you've made a mistake. I'm not a genie. I'm the most ordinary, normal, average girl you could meet. Ask anybody."

The genie didn't blink. "That's what all genies think," she replied, "until they turn twelve."

"*I* turned twelve," said Poppy, surprised.

"Just today."

"Yes, I know. That's why I'm here." Then the girl shot Poppy a cheeky smile and added, "Can't wait to see you in those funky new hiking boots, by the way."

Poppy stared. How did the girl know about the boots? They were hidden at the back of her closet!

"But I can't be a genie," Poppy insisted, shaking her head. "I'm—"

"You're Poppy Miller," interrupted the girl, pulling out a nail file and filing her already-perfect nails. "You got a B on your last math test. You were a tree in the school play. You have cheese and tomato sandwiches every day for lunch. You don't have a best friend and you pretend you don't care, but really you do. You feel like nothing exciting ever happens. And up until now, that's been true. But everything is about to change."

"Change?" asked Poppy, incredulous. "In what way?"

"In *every* way," said the girl. "As of today, you are expected to start behaving like a genie."

Poppy's legs suddenly felt very wobbly. She still didn't believe what this girl was saying. Not for a minute. But she also couldn't explain what was happening. She just wanted this girl to leave her alone!

"Look, you're wasting your time," said Poppy firmly. "I don't know anything about being a genie."

The girl put her nail file away. "Well, of course you don't!" she said. "That's why I'm here. I'm Lexie—your genie trainer."

Then Lexie picked up the bottle. "First off,

wearing the latest teenage genie fashion

female genies wear high ponytails, males wear turbans

perfectly manicured fingernails with gold nail polish

the more bangles you have, the more important you are

Lexie

Like all genies, Lexie likes to avoid granting wishes as much as possible.

we need to find a safe place to hide this," she said. "It would be very bad if someone found it accidentally."

"It'll be safe in the back of my closet," said Poppy. "That's my secret hiding spot—no one ever goes in there."

This wasn't exactly true. Astrid was always going through Poppy's closet and borrowing things. But Poppy was anxious to get this strange girl out of her room as quickly as possible.

Lexie raised her eyebrows. "OK, if you say so," she said, walking over to the closet and setting the bottle down inside of it. "Now we really need to go."

"*Go where?*" asked Poppy stubbornly.

"Into the genie bottle, of course!" replied Lexie.

Poppy looked down at the green bottle in the closet. Then she looked back at Lexie. "Listen,

Lexie," she said. "What you've said is all very interesting. And it's true that I have squeezed into some very small spaces over the years. But I can tell you right now that there is absolutely *no way* I can fit into that tiny bottle."

"Of course you can," said Lexie. "I fit in there just fine and I'm taller than you. Stop making excuses!"

Poppy sighed in annoyance. It seemed that Lexie just wouldn't take no for an answer. *OK, I'll play along with her stupid game,* decided Poppy. *Lexie will soon see that I can't squeeze in there.*

So Poppy stretched out her foot and pretended to try and slip it into the bottle. "See?" she said, looking at Lexie.

But Lexie just nodded. "Not bad for your first time," she said, sounding quite impressed.

"Keep going."

Poppy looked down at the bottle, and saw to her surprise that her foot had actually disappeared inside it!

*Is it possible Lexie is right?* wondered Poppy, shocked. *Am I actually a genie after all?*

But the moment Poppy thought about it, she found she couldn't squeeze in any further. Unfortunately, she also couldn't remove her foot!

"I'm stuck," she yelped, hopping around.

"You're trying too hard now," said Lexie. "Relax. Imagine that you're sand, pouring through an hourglass. Or water, flowing out of a tap."

This sounded crazy to Poppy. But it was hard to talk about anything being crazy when your foot was stuck in a bottle!

*I'm water. I'm sand. I'm sandy water. I'm watery sand,* thought Poppy, over and over again.

genies shrink up to $\frac{1}{20}$th of their normal size to fit in a bottle

whooosh!

not all genie bottles are fancy

genie bottles are hidden around the human world

some genies prefer plain bottles so as to attract less attention

favorite hiding spots are the back of the pantry, second-hand shops and sheds

# Genie bottle

At first, nothing happened. And then, all of a sudden, Poppy felt an odd tingling sensation in her foot, which was followed by a whooshy kind of feeling, like she was hurtling down a very tall building in a very fast elevator. So Poppy did what any normal, average person would do in this situation. She shut her eyes.

Finally, she felt a bump and the whooshiness stopped. A moment later, Poppy opened her eyes and found herself in a room that glowed green like a jewel.

*I must be inside the bottle,* thought Poppy, shaking her head in amazement. Which is not the sort of place that average, ordinary people usually find themselves.

# Chapter 3

Poppy couldn't resist having a little poke around the bottle.

Her bedroom at home was perfectly comfortable, but a little boring. Sometimes, when she couldn't sleep, Poppy would imagine what her perfect bedroom would look like. Then she would drift to sleep, pretending she was in that room.

Well, the inside of the bottle looked *exactly* like her dream bedroom!

The floor was covered with a thick, soft green carpet dotted with flowers. In the middle of the room was a huge bed, covered with colorful satin pillows. Draped over the bed was a sky-blue canopy, decorated with twinkling silver stars and moons. There was also a bookshelf shaped like a wave that was stocked with Poppy's favorite books and magazines. And one of Poppy's most favorite songs was playing, although Poppy couldn't tell where the music was coming from.

Just then, there was a puff of purple smoke and Lexie appeared. "So?" she said, looking around. "What do you think?"

"I love it!" said Poppy. "It's exactly how I would design my perfect bedroom."

"Well, of course it is," replied Lexie. "This is your bottle, after all."

stacks of stripy and spotty pillows

stars and moons canopy

huge bed!

colorful floor

thick flower carpet

# Inside the bottle

"*My* bottle?" said Poppy, surprised. "But *you* popped out of it."

"I was just delivering it to you," explained Lexie. "You get your own personal bottle, so you can decorate it however you like."

## DID YOU KNOW?

Some genies like their bottles to be very ornate, with lots of curtains and floor cushions. Other genies prefer to make their rooms look like something completely different—like a treehouse or a submarine. Note: It is not recommended to put a spa or a pool in a genie bottle, as the water sloshes everywhere if the bottle is picked up.

Once she knew this was her bottle, Poppy really wanted to have a better look around, but Lexie wouldn't let her.

"We have to get to the training center," Lexie said.

"How do we get there?" asked Poppy.

Lexie smiled and produced what looked like a small, rusty teapot. "With this," she replied.

"With an old *teapot*?" said Poppy, surprised.

"It's not a teapot," corrected Lexie. "It's a Location Lamp. Genies use them to get around. This one might look a little beaten up, but that just means that the lamp has been in use for centuries and is very reliable. I'll show you how it works."

Then Lexie twisted the lamp's lid. Instantly, a plume of pinkish smoke curled out of the spout and began forming into curly, smoky letters. Lexie started flicking the words around with her hand, like she was searching for something.

special coordinates, go wherever you like!

jewels act as extra buttons

Location Lamp

"Training center, training center," she muttered.

"Can I help?" asked Poppy politely.

"Thanks, but it's pretty complicated," said Lexie.

Then something odd happened. Two of the smoky words separated themselves from the jumble of letters hovering above the lamp and zoomed over to Poppy! She looked at the words in surprise:

### Training Center

"Um, excuse me, Lexie," said Poppy. "Is this what you're looking for?"

Lexie stared at the words in Poppy's hand. "Where did you find them?" she asked, clearly astonished.

"I didn't," said Poppy with a shrug. "They found me."

Lexie didn't look upset exactly, but for a

moment she had a very strange expression on her face. Then she touched the words like a button. "Let's go then. Oh, and get ready," she warned. "This can be a wild ride."

As Lexie finished speaking, everything went dark. Then the floor dropped away and Poppy once again found herself whooshing along through blackness, wondering how much weirder this day could possibly get.

Her mind insisted that this was all a dream. *But if it IS a dream, then I'll wake up soon enough*, she reminded herself. *So I may as well just go with it and see what happens!*

Lexie and Poppy twisted and looped through the air. Then, just when Poppy thought she wouldn't survive another second of it, the ride came to an abrupt stop. And Poppy promptly fell flat on her face!

*How embarrassing*, thought Poppy, jumping to her feet and dusting herself off. *I hope no one saw that.* But she was out of luck. Lexie was standing beside her looking calm and unruffled, and behind Lexie was a group of three kids—two girls and a boy, who all looked about twelve years old. The kids were all staring at Poppy like she was the weirdest thing they'd ever seen.

"What? Haven't you ever seen someone fall over?" said Poppy, putting her hands on her hips. "If you pay me a dollar, I'll do it again!"

Everyone laughed. The fair-haired girl near the front of the group smiled apologetically.

"Sorry for staring," she said, sticking her hand out for Poppy to shake. "I'm Rose. Don't feel dumb about falling over. We all did exactly the same thing. I guess we're all new to this genie stuff."

Poppy instantly felt less angry. This girl seemed nice.

"Hang on, *I* didn't fall," corrected a dark-haired boy. "Which probably means I'm a super-genie or something."

Poppy scrutinized the boy through narrowed eyes. He was wearing a grubby old football sweatshirt, beaten-up jeans, and scruffy sneakers. He looked like the kind of boy who girls at Poppy's school always had crushes on, although Poppy could never see why.

"A super-doofus, more likely," she said under her breath.

Rose and the other girl laughed.

The boy glared at Poppy. "What did you say?" he demanded.

But just then Lexie clapped her hands.

"Hey, enough chat. You've got plenty of time to get to know each other," she said. "Find a seat and we'll start."

Poppy looked around. Lexie had called this place the training center, which sounded like a school. But this place didn't look like a school. The room had the same curved walls as her bedroom bottle. It didn't smell like a school either—it smelled like hot toast with jam. And there were no tables and chairs to be seen, just big, soft floor cushions and luxurious Persian carpets.

"Are we supposed to sit on the cushions?" wondered Poppy out loud.

"Well, duh. Of *course*!" said the boy in the football sweatshirt. "You didn't think genies would have normal desks, did you?"

"I have no idea," retorted Poppy, plonking herself down on an emerald green cushion. "That's why I'm here—to *learn* stuff. Why are you here, if you're already such an expert?"

The boy opened his mouth to reply, but to Poppy's delight, Lexie spoke before he got a chance.

### DID YOU KNOW?

Everything in the Genie Realm is inside a bottle—even the gardens and beaches. Once you are outside a bottle, you are back in the normal world.

"I want you all to picture yourselves this morning," Lexie said. "What you felt like. How you looked. Who you thought you were."

Everyone nodded.

"Now, forget all of it," said Lexie. "You're not that person anymore. Today, you've all become trainee genies. You are different from your family and friends. You are out of the ordinary. In fact, you are *extraordinary*."

Poppy felt a little shiver of excitement when Lexie said that. It was pretty cool having someone say that she wasn't ordinary.

But Lexie's next words brought Poppy back to earth.

"Of course, you're all a long way off being fully fledged genies," she said. "You might not be normal humans—or normies, as we call them—but none of you are capable of granting wishes yet. You're somewhere in between. In the Genie Realm, we call you guys *tweenie genies*. And if you don't listen to me and do what I say, you won't ever get past this stage," she added sternly. "It's very rare for every tweenie in a class to graduate. The odds are that at least one of you will fail."

Everyone looked shocked. It wasn't a nice thing to hear. To make it even worse, the boy with the football sweatshirt smirked at Poppy.

"She's talking about you!" he whispered. "Because you're more like a teeny weeny than a tweenie genie."

Poppy rolled her eyes and turned away, but inside she was seething. *How rude!* Sure, she wasn't tall, but she definitely wasn't teeny weeny.

*I'll show that boy!* she decided. *And I'll show Lexie, too. I'm going to be the best tweenie genie anyone has ever seen!*

# Chapter 4

Lexie pulled out a pile of red backpacks from a sliding panel in the floor of the Training Center Bottle.

"These are your tweenie genie kits," she explained, handing them out. "They're packed with useful stuff."

Each bag had the tweenie's name on the back in gold lettering. Poppy noticed that the boy's bag had **Jake** written on it. She quickly looked away and busied herself with her own backpack. The less she knew about that irritating boy, the better!

The first thing she pulled out of her bag was a silver bangle, like the ones Lexie wore. She slipped it on straightaway.

Lexie nodded. "That's right. You must all wear your tweenie bangle at all times. And yes," she said, turning to the boy, "that means you too, Jake."

Poppy saw Jake scowl as he slipped the bangle on.

"You should all have one of these in your backpacks," Lexie continued, holding up a book with a hard purple cover and a silver pen clipped on the side. "It's a genie jotter. Use it to take notes. And when you need them, important lessons will appear in it, too."

Poppy opened hers up and stroked the

creamy, blank pages admiringly. *It's like a diary,* she thought.

"Mine won't open," called the other girl, whose bag had **Hazel** written on it.

"Of course not," said Lexie. "Stage One tweenies always need the key to open the diaries. The bangle is actually the key, so press it against the cover to open the diary."

"Um, Lexie?" said Poppy nervously. "Mine opened without the key."

Lexie frowned. "That's impossible! Show me."

So Poppy closed the diary and then opened it again, feeling a little silly. Then Lexie gave Poppy the same strange, intense look that she'd given her when the Location Lamp words zoomed to her hand. It was like she was searching her face for something.

Poppy flushed. "Am I in trouble?" she

46

jotter can only be opened with a bangle key

if anyone else tries to write in it, the ink won't stick to the pages

Poppy Miller: Twenie Genie

has built-in spell checker

only this pen will write in the jotter

words appear when the genie needs the information

# Genie jotter

asked nervously.

"No," said Lexie quietly. "But in the future, please use the key, OK?"

"OK," muttered Poppy. It felt dumb using a key when the diary opened up perfectly by itself. But she could tell there was no point arguing.

Hazel shot her a look of sympathy, and Rose whispered kindly, "It's not your fault. You didn't know."

Then Jake leaned over. "Teeny Weeny broke the jotter! Teeny Weeny broke the jotter!" he sang softly.

Some things just didn't deserve a reply, so Poppy ignored him. Then she unclipped the silver pen and wrote her name on the first page. She couldn't help smiling then. How good it looked!

"Are there any questions?" asked Lexie.

The tweenies all looked at each other and then shot up their hands. Of course there were!

Hazel went first. "Why did we get chosen to be genies?" she asked.

"You didn't get *chosen*," said Lexie. "You are genies because you all have the Genie Gene. The Genie Gene is very rare. So when you're born with it, we watch you until you're ready to join the Genie Realm. Your genie powers don't actually start working until you're twelve, so we don't bother telling you about your real identity until then."

"Does that mean our families aren't genies?" asked Poppy.

Lexie nodded. "That's right," she said. "Although sometimes there is more than one genie in a family. That's very rare, though."

"Are we the *only* tweenie genies?" asked Rose.

"Oh, no," said Lexie. "There are other groups of tweenies being trained by other trainers right now. But we like to train you in small groups to start with. You'll meet up with other tweenies in the later stages of your training."

"How long does training go for?" Jake asked.

"You have just started Stage One," explained Lexie. "It's like a crash course in genie stuff, just to get you on the right track. Stage One goes for three nights. You'll come here every evening, study all night, and return to your normie families each morning."

"So, when exactly do we sleep?" asked Jake, sounding puzzled.

"There won't be any time for sleep," said Lexie firmly. "But don't worry. You'll get nap breaks."

Lexie paced around the room. "During the next three days, you will learn about our rules and customs. You'll learn how to act and how to look, and hopefully, how to feel like a genie. Then, at the end of the week, there will be an examination."

### DID YOU KNOW?

Sleeping in a genie bottle is much better than sleeping in a normie bed. The air is super-concentrated, so fifteen minutes of genie bottle sleep is worth two hours of normie sleep.

"What kind of examination?" asked Jake.

"The first part is a written exam," explained Lexie. Then she held up a thick book with a red cover and gold-edged pages. "This is our *Genie History and Culture* textbook. You'll need to know it back-to-front for the exam."

Poppy gulped. When were they supposed to get time to read a book that big if they were at normie school all day and genie school all night? She could tell from the other tweenies' faces that she wasn't the only one wondering.

But Lexie had already moved on. "The second part of the exam is more like a ball," she continued. "It takes place in the Ballroom at the Genie Palace Bottle. That's where you'll be presented to the Genie Royal Family and will have to demonstrate everything you've learned so far. If you pass both parts of the exam, you are allowed to go on to Stage Two of tweenie genie training. That's when you go to one of the big genie schools with all the other Stage Two tweenies."

"And is that the end of the training?" asked Poppy, feeling a little overwhelmed.

"Not quite," said Lexie. "After that comes the most difficult part of all, Stage Three. I'm not even going to start talking about that right now, because it'll scare you. But if you get through that—and believe me, that's a big *if*—then you'll be fully qualified."

No one said anything for a moment. Then Rose asked the exact question that Poppy had been thinking. "What happens if we don't pass Stage One?"

Lexie's voice was quiet, but matter-of-fact. "You'll be returned to your old life, with your memory wiped clear of all genie stuff."

Poppy bit her lip. There was no way she wanted that to happen!

Then Hazel raised her hand. "So can we call our families and tell them where we are?" She looked a little homesick.

"Definitely not!" Lexie said, looking shocked. "That would be breaking the first Genie Golden Law. You must not tell any normie that you are a genie."

"Oh," said Hazel, looking like she might cry.

Now it was Poppy's turn to give Hazel a sympathetic look. *How was she supposed to know that?* thought Poppy. *It's not like it's written down anywhere.* But then Poppy glanced at her jotter and saw something very surprising. What had been a completely blank page a moment ago now had golden writing on it:

★ **Golden Law # 1:**
Do not reveal your identity to anyone.

"But won't our families wonder where we've gone at night?" said Hazel, her voice wobbling a bit.

"Oh, don't worry about that," said Lexie. "It's been taken care of. Your houses and schools have all been fitted with an Excuse Generator which starts working the moment you enter the Genie Realm. It will cover for you."

"When do we get our wands?" asked Rose eagerly.

## DID YOU KNOW?

The Excuse Generator is a top secret device that keeps normie families distracted when a genie is called away on genie business. It fits in the base of a telephone and when an excuse is required, the Excuse Generator will call. It can imitate hundreds of different voices and is highly believable.

Lexie burst out laughing. "Genies don't *have* wands. They use special moves to grant wishes. It's like sign language. Except that every genie works out his or her own special combination of hand movements."

"That sounds like dancing," frowned Jake. "And I don't dance."

"Well, if you want to be a genie, you'll have to learn," replied Lexie. "But don't worry. Even if you don't like doing that part of your training, there are other parts I think you'll definitely enjoy. Let me demonstrate."

Then Lexie sat down cross-legged on the ground and closed her eyes. The tweenies watched her curiously. Was she meditating? Poppy was definitely not expecting what happened next. . . .

Lexie began rising up into the air, until

she was hovering a foot off the ground!

"Are we really going to learn how to do that?" asked Hazel excitedly as Lexie floated gracefully back down. Suddenly, she didn't look quite so homesick.

"Well, you'll have to, if you want to pass the test," said Lexie, grinning.

"That is going to be so much fun!" said Hazel. "As well as granting wishes, of course."

"Actually, granting wishes can be a bit of

a pain," admitted Lexie. "One minute, you're relaxing in your bottle, and then *whoosh!* Suddenly, you're plonked in front of some irritating normie who starts demanding all kinds of stupid stuff they don't need. The best genies are the ones who get out of granting wishes as much as possible."

*I don't believe that,* Poppy thought. *Granting wishes HAS to be fun!*

"And you'll all need to memorize the second Golden Law," added Lexie.

Poppy looked down at her open genie jotter. More words had appeared:

### ★ Golden Law # 2:
Tweenies are not allowed to grant wishes until they have passed their first examination.

Then Lexie clapped her hands, her bangles

jangling like chimes. "That'll do for now," she said. "Let's go into town. To start feeling like genies, you need to start looking like genies. You guys need a complete style overhaul. Hair, clothes, the works."

"You mean just the girls, right?" asked Jake hopefully.

But Lexie shook her head. "Everyone," she said. "There's no way you can learn to be a real genie in that dirty old football sweatshirt, Jake."

Poppy couldn't help laughing at Jake's horrified face. *Well,* she thought. *At least Jake and I have ONE thing in common. We both hate makeovers!*

# Chapter 5

Lexie showed the tweenies how to use their Location Lamps. "We're going to the Emerald Mall. It's one of the biggest shopping bottles in the Genie Realm," she explained. "When we arrive, stay close to me and don't wander off. It's a pretty crazy place."

Poppy twisted the top of her lamp until the smoky words appeared. She clicked on Emerald Mall.

*Here goes*! thought Poppy, bracing herself.

Just like before, the floor seemed to drop away and Poppy found herself spinning and looping through the air.

*It doesn't seem so fast this time*, thought Poppy, relieved. *Or maybe I'm getting used to it!*

Poppy heard the Emerald Mall before she saw it. It sounded like a thousand bees humming in a field. She carefully opened her eyes and gasped. The Emerald Mall was inside a bottle that was as big as a skyscraper and so wide that Poppy couldn't even see the sides. The whole place was alive with action.

The bottom of the bottle was filled with tiny shops and brightly colored stalls, all packed together so tightly that Poppy couldn't see how you could squeeze past without knocking something over. Genies were bustling about, examining trinkets and haggling with the shopkeepers.

But the most remarkable thing was that the shops weren't just on the ground level. Hundreds of shops were floating around in the air! The Emerald Mall was definitely like nothing Poppy had ever seen. Even Jake looked impressed.

"Lexie, how do you get up to those floating shops?" asked Poppy curiously.

"By magic carpet, of course," replied Lexie. As she spoke, a passing genie whistled shrilly and a small, red carpet zipped over to him instantly, nearly knocking Poppy over!

The carpet dropped to the ground and the waiting genie stepped on. Then the carpet zoomed off again toward one of the floating shops.

"Can we have a turn on one of those?" asked Jake eagerly.

"No way!" exclaimed Lexie. "You wouldn't

be able to control a magic carpet yet."

## DID YOU KNOW?

Magic carpets are one of the most popular forms of
transportation in the genie world, although there
are others—such as flying bikes (called "flikes").

"Can we have a look around?" asked Rose.

Lexie shook her head. "No time today, I'm
afraid," she said. "We have appointments to
keep. I'll just have to give you a running
commentary as we go."

Lexie took off at top speed, winding her way
between the busy market stalls and genie shop-
pers.

"I can see what she means about a *running*

commentary," muttered Jake.

Poppy couldn't help laughing. Jake was right. Lexie didn't slow down for a second as she pointed out the sights.

"To your left, you'll see the shoemakers" shops. You've probably noticed that genie shoes curl over at the top. This is to help us hook onto things like tree branches if we need to make an emergency stop while levitating or on a magic carpet," Lexie said. "And on your right are the wigmakers' shops. Girl genies all wear high ponytails, so the wigmakers provide hair extensions for tweenie genies whose hair is too short. Hazel, you'll need some."

The air filled with delicious smells. "Now, we're coming into the food court," said Lexie. "Genies love spicy food, and we also love things that are unusual and surprising. A popular snack in the Genie Realm is spicy springballs. They look like mini meatballs, but rather than just sitting on a plate, they spring into your mouth all on their own. This is totally fine if you're expecting it, but it can be a choking hazard if you're not."

Sure enough, the group soon passed a genie holding a plate of tiny meatballs. He opened his mouth and right away, the springballs started leaping into his mouth!

## DID YOU KNOW?

Genie sandwiches are completely different than normie ones. For one thing, genies NEVER eat crusts—and it is considered the height of rudeness to serve a genie a sandwich where the crusts have not been removed.

Poppy was feeling a bit exhausted when Lexie finally stopped in front of a funny, dark little shop at the end of a narrow lane. The gold letters on the front window said that they had arrived at Madame di Silver's Fashion Emporium. Inside, Lexie introduced them to Madame herself.

"You should feel honored, tweenies," she said. "Madame is the finest dressmaker in the entire Genie Realm. She even makes clothes for the Genie Royal Family."

"Welcome to my shop!" said Madame, who was an elegantly dressed genie with a broad smile. "I'll get you all looking like genie princesses in no time."

"Not all of us, I hope," Jake said, horrified.

But Madame didn't seem to hear him. She pulled out some shimmery blue genie pants and a gold top and held it up against Poppy.

"What about something like this?" Madame suggested. "Maybe paired with some gold sequined slippers?"

Now, Poppy usually hated shopping. And she detested people picking out clothes for her. But this was completely different. These clothes were exactly the sort of thing she'd always longed to wear—unusual and beautiful and not at all like Clothes Club clothes!

She looked pleadingly at Lexie. But Lexie shook her head.

"Sorry, but no," she said firmly. "Just the regulation tweenie uniforms and pajamas today. The tweenies can come back for fancy stuff when they're getting ready for the Graduation Ball."

Madame smiled apologetically at Poppy

67

and then pulled out a stack of white garments for each of the tweenies.

Once she had changed, Poppy looked down at the uniform and half smiled, half sighed. They were very beautiful genie clothes, but *totally* boring and simple compared with the clothes Madame di Silver had first selected!

But Lexie was very pleased. "Much better!" she declared, looking at the group. "Now for your hair." She ushered the tweenies through a curtain at the back of the shop where they found Madame's hairdressing salon.

"All the girls will be shown how to do the proper high genie ponytails," she explained. "And you," she added, looking at Jake, "will be fitted with a training turban."

The hair salon was so small that only two genies could be attended to at a time.

Poppy and Jake were first. Poppy, much to her surprise, mastered the art of pulling her hair into a high ponytail fairly easily. For once, she was happy to have boring, straight hair, because she could tell it would be much harder to do with curls like Rose's or short hair like Hazel's. Then she caught a glimpse of Jake. He was wearing a magnificent green turban.

"You look like a *real* genie!" giggled Poppy.

"Yeah, well so do you, Teeny Weeny," Jake snorted.

"Very good," said Lexie approvingly, looking Poppy and Jake up and down. "Now, you two wait out front while the others get their hair done. But don't wander away!"

*I'll just pretend Jake isn't here,* decided Poppy, sitting down on the step in front of the shop. There were plenty of interesting things in the street to distract her from the most annoying boy who ever existed! Genies were zooming by on magic carpets, carrying interesting packages and eating delicious-smelling snacks.

*I wish I could go exploring,* thought Poppy longingly, as two genies flew past carrying what looked like steaming-hot ice cream.

Then Jake nudged her, a mischievous gleam in his eye. "I heard Madame say that Rose and Hazel both have tricky hair, so they'll be in there for ages," he said. "If we're quick, we could have a look around and be back before Lexie even notices."

Poppy hesitated. It was very tempting, but she didn't really trust Jake. He was so annoying

70

turban

high ponytail

curly shoes

¾ length pants

Uniform

that he'd probably abandon her somewhere, and then rat on her to Lexie.

## DID YOU KNOW?

Genie hair is half the thickness of normal human hair, but they have twice the amount. It also grows at double the speed!

*But if I don't go, who knows when I'll get a chance to come back?* Poppy reminded herself. *Although, I really don't want to get into trouble....*

She was just about to tell Jake no when a genie not much older than themselves rode past on a bicycle—in midair!

Poppy stood up. "Right," she said. "Let's go!"

Poppy and Jake began wandering through the narrow market lanes. One shop had a giant fish tank instead of a window. Tiny, jewel-like fish flittered about, one minute covered with spots and the next with stripes. Poppy tapped gently on the glass and to her astonishment, one of the fish turned and roared at her like a tiger!

"I guess that's to scare you," laughed Jake.

"Well, it works really well," Poppy grinned, her heartbeat gradually returning to normal.

Around another corner they saw a juggler. Poppy had seen jugglers before, of course. But she'd never seen one whose objects kept changing! One minute he was juggling a ball, a vase, and an umbrella. But a moment later, he was juggling a lollipop, a ukulele, and a wriggling snake!

They saw a market stand selling fruit that

looked like oranges, but the flesh inside was purple. Another shop sold lollipops shaped like butterflies that flew around the shop, dusting everything with sugar as they went. Genies were chasing them around with long-handled nets.

As Poppy and Jake watched, a couple of the butterflies flew out the shop door toward them.

"Catch them!" yelled Poppy, grabbing and missing.

Then Jake leapt up and somehow managed to scoop them up with his turban. "Here you go," he said, offering them to the candy store owner who was standing in the doorway.

The shop owner smiled. "First time at the Emerald Mall?" he said kindly.

Poppy and Jake nodded.

"You can have them, then," he said.

"Thanks," grinned Jake.

Then Jake did something really nice. He gave one of the butterflies to Poppy!

"Thanks," she said, quickly popping it in her mouth before he changed his mind. It fizzled on her tongue like sherbet.

"See," said Jake cheerfully, like he was reading her mind. "I'm not totally annoying *all* the time."

Poppy smiled back. It was true that Jake seemed less irritating all of a sudden. In fact, Poppy was enjoying herself so much that she completely forgot the time. It wasn't until she heard a clock chiming that she checked her watch and gasped in horror. They'd been gone for ages!

"We've got to get back," she said urgently. "Which way?"

"Don't ask me," said Jake, shrugging. "I'm lost."

Poppy stared at him in dismay. "What are we going to do?"

"I don't know," replied Jake. "Only a magic carpet would get us to Madame di Silver's in time."

*He's right,* thought Poppy. *A magic carpet would definitely be the fastest way to travel. Even though Lexie did say that tweenies can't control magic carpets. . . .*

That exact moment, a magic carpet zoomed past and Poppy let out a piercing whistle. To both tweenies' astonishment, the carpet

carpets are used as elevators when genies don't feel like levitating

they are used to carry things like food and luggage

never wipe your feet on a magic carpet! They hate it!

food is often served on top of them

lint and dust weighs a carpet down so it can't fly

# Magic carpet

screeched to a stop. Then it did a U-turn and landed at Poppy's feet, twitching its tassels.

"Climb on!" Poppy told Jake.

Jake put one foot on the carpet, which promptly slid out from under him. "Hey! That carpet totally did that on purpose!" he exclaimed, toppling over. "It's got a nasty streak. Just look at the way it's flapping its corners."

"Don't be ridiculous," said Poppy. "It's perfectly friendly." She wasn't sure why, but somehow she just knew that the carpet wouldn't try the same trick on her. And sure enough, she stepped onto it easily.

"Come on!" she urged Jake.

"No way, Teeny Weeny!" protested Jake. "That rug is insane. Plus, you don't have a clue how to drive it."

Poppy shrugged. "Either you get on, or

78

you figure out a way to explain where you've been to Lexie."

"Good point," said Jake, jumping on.

At first, the magic carpet did nothing at all. Poppy stared down anxiously.

"See, I knew you wouldn't be able to work it," said Jake.

But Poppy wasn't giving up so easily. *Maybe it's waiting for instructions*, she thought. So in a loud, confident voice, she said, "Please, take us to Madame di Silver's shop."

Instantly, the carpet obediently rose from the ground and took off at top speed. Poppy and Jake held on as tightly as they could!

"Looks like I can fly this thing after all," Poppy shouted over the noise of the wind.

"Beginner's luck!" laughed Jake as they zoomed along.

"I don't think so!" Poppy retorted. She quickly worked out that she could steer the carpet by leaning one way or another. *I wonder what will happen if I pull on the tassels?*

She gave one a gentle tug and the carpet began zooming straight up.

"Better hold on!" yelled Poppy, and the carpet did a complete loop.

"OK, OK," Jake half laughed, half gasped. "I take it all back. You *do* know how to drive it. Just no more loops, all right?"

The carpet dropped Poppy and Jake outside Madame di Silver's shop and then rose up again, ready to take off. Poppy felt a bit sad. She'd become very fond of the carpet.

"Thanks for the ride," she said to the carpet,

giving it a pat.

The carpet did a couple of loops around her, and tickled her cheek with a tassel.

"Off you go before Lexie sees us, you oversized doormat," muttered Jake.

The carpet flew over and slapped him on the nose with a corner.

"Ouch!" spluttered Jake, as the carpet sped off. "Right. That's it. I'm walking everywhere from now on. These carpets are nutso."

They had arrived back just in time. The shop door swung open and Lexie appeared, followed by Rose and Hazel with their new genie ponytails.

"Where have you been?" Lexie asked Poppy and Jake, her eyebrows raised. "I looked out the window a minute ago and you weren't there."

Poppy swallowed. There was no way she

could lie to Lexie. She opened her mouth to blurt out the truth, but Jake jumped in first.

"Sorry, Lexie. I wandered off, and Poppy came and got me," he said.

Poppy looked at him in disbelief. Had Jake just lied to get her out of trouble?

"I can kick you out of tweenie genie training at any stage, Jake," said Lexie sternly.

Jake's face went red and Poppy found herself feeling sorry for him. Lexie was scary when she was angry.

"It won't happen again," said Jake meekly.

When Lexie had turned away, Poppy whispered awkwardly, "You didn't have to do that. But thanks."

Jake shrugged. "I figured you'd been in enough trouble this morning," he said, "and anyway, it was worth it. I had loads of fun!

Didn't you?"

Poppy thought about all the amazing things they'd seen at the Emerald Mall, with its dazzling colors and smells and genies. And then she thought about how nice it had been wandering around with Jake. It was almost like ... well, like Jake had turned into a friend in the mall.

"Yes," admitted Poppy with a big smile. "I really did."

# Chapter 6

Lexie gathered the newly styled tweenie genies around her.

"Good work, guys," she said, smiling. "Time to take a break in your genie bottles. But be back at the training center in an hour. We've got loads more to get through tonight."

Poppy was very glad to hear they were getting a break. She was very tired and even an hour's rest would be good. She said good-bye to the others and used her lamp to get back to her genie bottle. And this time she didn't even fall over when she landed!

Before she climbed into bed, Poppy checked the clothes that Madame di Silver had given her. Sure enough, she found a pair of white, fluffy pajamas, soft as a cloud.

As she pulled her blanket up, Poppy noticed a dial on the headboard with different settings, including Magic Carpet and Waterbed.

*I've had enough riding on magic carpets for one evening*, Poppy smiled to herself, so she changed the setting to Waterbed. Instantly, the green carpet seemed to disappear and was replaced by what looked like gently rolling waves. The sound of a sea breeze rose up around her, and it felt for all the world like the bed was a snug little boat, rocking to and fro on the sea.

Poppy woke feeling refreshed and alert. But to her surprise, the clock said that it was only an hour later. Poppy got changed back into her uniform and grabbed her Location Lamp.

When she arrived at the Training Center, she saw that it had been set up for a feast. In the middle of the room were large carpets laden with food. As soon as Poppy sat down, one of the carpets floated over to her, waiting patiently while she picked something to eat. She chose a bowl of pink yogurt sprinkled with bright green pistachios and a plate of mini blueberry pancakes, each with a blob of strawberry jam on top.

Across the other side of the Training Center Bottle, Poppy saw Jake drinking a bottle of juice through a very curly straw. As the juice traveled up the straw, it changed color. It started off orange, then changed to pink half way up, and was purple by the time it reached the top!

When snack time was finished and the carpets had whisked the dirty plates away, there was a puff of purple smoke and Lexie appeared.

"Grab your jotters, everyone," she said. "I'm going to teach you about Wish Twisting."

Poppy's jotter fell open to a blank page. But as Poppy watched, words appeared.

### How to Twist a Wish

★ **Step 1**: Generally, normies make terrible wishes. Try to talk them out of the whole thing.

★ **Step 2**: Try looking for the loophole so you can get out of granting it.

★ **Step 3:** If this doesn't work, grant them their wish, but add a twist!

★ **Step 4:** If all else fails, remember that sometimes just granting the normie exactly what they wish for is enough to make them never want another wish.

"I don't understand Step 3," said Poppy. "What does *add a twist* mean?"

Jake's hand shot up. "I bet it means that if the normie wishes to be tall, you make them mega-tall—like a skyscraper or something. Or if they wish to be rich, you turn them into a gooey chocolate cake, covered in cream. Or if they wish—"

"OK, I get it!" said Poppy, laughing. "So, if they wish they could fly, I give them a plane ticket."

Lexie nodded approvingly. "Exactly," she said. "Genies are bound by ancient genie law to grant wishes. But that doesn't mean we can't do it in our own way."

Then Lexie clapped her hands. "OK, now that we've covered the basics of Wish Twisting, let's move onto Wish *Granting*."

Poppy felt a shiver of excitement. Now *this* sounded more like it!

"Why are you teaching us Wish Granting at all," asked Jake, "if we're supposed to just try and get out of it?"

"Well, there are some normies who make good wishes that you want to grant," explained Lexie. "And there are other times when you have no option but to grant a wish, regardless of how silly it is. And to do that, you'll need to come up with your own personal wish routine. No one can teach it to you. It's something you have to discover for yourself. All I can do is show you some basic wish moves. Then it's up to you."

"How will we know when we've worked it out?" asked Hazel.

"If your routine is correct, you'll see a puff of smoke rise up from the ground around your feet," replied Lexie.

Lexie double-clapped her hands and some very fast, very fun music began playing. "Most tweenies find it easier to learn these wish movements to music," she said.

## DID YOU KNOW?

Genies only like music that has a strong rhythm and a fast beat. If they can't dance to it, they simply aren't interested!

Poppy could understand why. You couldn't help but dance to the genie music. Even Jake was tapping his foot!

Lexie started by showing them some simple moves. There was one where their hands twisted around like snakes. And there was another tricky one where they pointed one foot at their knee and spun around with their hands held above their heads. Once they mastered a move, Lexie moved onto another one right away. Poppy had to really concentrate to keep up.

When they knew about twenty moves, Lexie said, "OK, it's over to you guys now. Play around with the steps and see if you can come up with anything. Usually, these basic moves will be enough. But sometimes, you have to add a special movement all your own to get your routine right. That's when things can get tricky."

snake
hands

head
nod

hip
swivel

ankle
pivot

# Wish routine

But sometimes the genie needs to add a special move all of her own.

The tweenies all found their own space, and started practicing the moves. It seemed like they'd only been practicing for five minutes when Jake gave an excited shout.

"I've worked mine out!" he said.

Poppy frowned. *There's no way he could've come up with one so quickly,* she thought. *He doesn't even like dancing!*

Everyone crowded around Jake. He folded his arms and tapped his foot in and out. Then he did a funny hip-wiggle. Everyone laughed. Poppy knew they were all thinking the same thing. There was no way that Jake's routine could be right. It was way too simple!

Jake finished the routine by jumping down onto one knee and bowing his head. Then, to Poppy's astonishment, a puff of yellow smoke shot up from the ground beneath him.

"Nice work, Jake," smiled Lexie, giving him a pat on the back.

Even though she and Jake were friends now, Poppy felt a tiny bit jealous. She would've loved to be the first one to work out her routine. Then Lexie would be patting *her* on the back and smiling.

*I'll be the next to finish*, Poppy told herself determinedly. Her routine felt like it was fairly close to completion. It started with a snake hands move, followed by a double spin and a slide. All she needed was a way to wrap it up.

But Poppy wasn't the next to finish. Hazel was next, then Rose. Then finally Lexie ended the class.

"Nice work tweenies," she said. "I've never had a group that got their routines down so quickly. And don't worry, Poppy, you'll get yours, too. Just work on it in your spare time."

Poppy wanted to say, "What spare time?" But instead she asked, "What happens if I can't work it out?"

Lexie hesitated, and then said, "You won't graduate. But that's not even the worse thing that could happen. What would be far worse is if a normie found your bottle and tried to make a wish. That's why we made sure your bottle was hidden somewhere safe before we left the normie world."

Lexie turned back to the rest of the class. "That's it for today," she said. "You can all head back to your normie families now."

The other tweenies started packing up their things. But Poppy stood still, fixed to the spot. She knew perfectly well that her closet wasn't a safe hiding spot at all! Just the thought of it made her feel queasy. She had to get back there before Astrid walked in.

"Hey, you look really strange," said Jake, watching her curiously. "Stranger than you usually do, I mean!"

Poppy shook her head. She *felt* strange. Too strange even to come up with a smart comeback to Jake. Her fingers and toes had pins and needles. She saw Jake mouthing something, but she couldn't hear him. And then she felt like she had turned into an icy cold milkshake and someone was sucking her up through a straw. It was most unpleasant. Poppy shut her eyes and hoped the feeling would pass quickly. . . .

*WHOOSH!* Poppy suddenly felt like she'd fallen out of bed onto the floor. She opened her eyes and looked around. She was back in her bedroom. And standing in front of her was Astrid.

"Oh my gosh!" said Astrid, her eyes wide. "You're a *genie!* And I am *so* telling Mom and Dad!"

# Chapter 7

**M**onday, October 18th, 8am

"What are you doing in my closet, Astrid?" asked Poppy, trying to act like there was nothing strange about suddenly popping out of a bottle.

"Mom told me to come and get you for breakfast," said Astrid, "and also I need to borrow your new hiking boots."

"You came to snoop around, more likely,"

said Poppy crankily.

"Who cares," said Astrid dismissively. "We've got way more interesting things to talk about! Like, how long have you been a genie? Am I one, too? When do I get a wand? Mom and Dad are going to be so mad that you didn't tell them first! And we've finally found your special talent, little sis!"

Poppy felt herself growing more and more upset as Astrid talked. Being a genie was her own special secret! For a moment, Poppy thought about snatching the bottle out of her sister's hand and running away. But if the bottle smashed, she might not be able to get back to the Genie Realm!

So instead, Poppy tried to stay calm and said, "You can't tell anyone about this, Astrid, especially not

Mom and Dad. It'd be a big disaster if you did. So just hand me back my bottle, and we can forget all about this."

But Astrid held it up high, out of Poppy's reach. "I don't think so, little sis!" she said, waggling her finger in a very annoying way. "I want my three wishes. You're obviously a genie, and I found your bottle. So you owe me."

Suddenly, Poppy understood completely what Lexie meant about wish-granting not always being fun. Granting Astrid's wishes wouldn't be even slightly enjoyable. Plus, there was a huge problem. *I haven't got my wish routine worked out yet,* thought Poppy.

Then she remembered the wish twisting rules. *Can I try and talk Astrid out of making a wish?* she wondered. It was worth a try.

"Listen, Astrid," said Poppy, as sweetly as

she could. "I'm very new at this whole genie thing. I'm not even allowed to grant wishes yet. How about I write you a special genie I-O-U and maybe in a couple of years—"

"No way!" Astrid interrupted, shaking her head. "You're always trying to get out of stuff because you're the youngest, but I'm not letting that happen this time. I want my wishes or I'm telling Mom on you!"

"But I'm not sure that I even know how to grant one," said Poppy, irritated.

"Don't worry," said Astrid. "I'll start with an easy one."

"Oh yes, and what's that?" asked Poppy suspiciously.

"Easy," grinned Astrid. "I want to be super famous—the most famous person ever!"

"But you've already won loads of medals

and trophies," pointed out Poppy angrily. "Aren't you famous enough?"

But Astrid shook her head. "No way, sis," she smirked.

DID YOU KNOW?

These are the top five most common
wishes that normies make:

1. I wish for a million more wishes

2. I wish I were rich

3. I wish I were famous

4. I wish I didn't have to go to school anymore

5. I wish I could fly

Poppy knew she was in a tough spot. She had about as much chance of granting her sister's wish as she did of suddenly sprouting wings and flying around the room. But there was no way Astrid would give Poppy back the bottle unless she granted her wishes!

Then an idea popped into Poppy's head. *I'll just pretend that I've granted Astrid's wish,* she decided. *I'll tell her it won't work right away. Then, when she's not looking, I'll get the bottle back from her and find a MUCH better hiding place.* It was a risky plan, but Poppy didn't know what else she could do.

"OK, OK," Poppy said to Astrid, pretending to give in. "I'll grant your stupid wish if you promise not to tell anyone."

"Finally!" said Astrid smugly.

Poppy stood on her bed. She did the snake hands move, followed by a double spin. Then she did a slide and this time, ended the routine with a low bow. There was no puff of smoke, so she knew the routine still wasn't right, but that didn't matter. She just had to convince Astrid that she knew what she was doing.

"I grant Astrid's wish," Poppy said, in a loud, serious-sounding voice. "She will be the most famous person in the world!"

Then she and Astrid stood there, staring at each other.

"How can I tell if it's worked?" asked Astrid suspiciously.

"Of *course* it worked," said Poppy quickly. "It takes a while to kick in, that's all." Then she reached out her hand towards Astrid. "And now that I've granted your wish, please give me back my bottle."

"Nice try!" laughed Astrid, pulling the bottle away. "But I bet that if you get your hands on this thing, you'll disappear. Sorry Poppy, you're not going anywhere just yet."

104

Poppy could have screamed with frustration! *I'm stuck here until I find a way of getting my bottle back*, she realized grimly. *And that could take forever. . . .*

"Poppy! Astrid! Breakfast!" called their mom from the kitchen.

Astrid shoved the genie bottle into her schoolbag and flounced off down the hall.

Still feeling quite upset, Poppy quickly changed out of her genie uniform and into her school clothes. She was about to re-do her hair into its normal style when she stopped.

*No, I'll keep the high ponytail in*, she decided. *It'll remind me of who I really am.*

She kept her silver genie bangle on too, and slipped her schoolbooks into her red tweenie backpack. Then she went down to breakfast.

It was weird seeing her parents that morning. Even though it had been just over twelve hours since she last saw them, it felt like much longer. For them, nothing had changed. They were drinking tea and reading the paper, just like they did every morning. But for Poppy, everything had changed.

"So, Poppy," smiled her dad as she came in. "How was your first night as a tweenager?"

Poppy shrugged. "Not too bad," she said.

Her mom looked at her curiously. "You look different somehow, sweetie."

"It's probably just my new hairdo," Poppy replied quickly.

"No, that's not quite it," said her mom thoughtfully. "You just seem older."

"Well, she is older," said Poppy's dad, putting down his newspaper. "And that reminds me. Now that you're twelve, Poppy, we expect you to start doing a few more chores. You have to start *earning* that allowance."

"Does that mean I'll get a bit more?" asked Poppy hopefully.

"No," said her dad. "You get quite enough for someone your age."

"You need to take your schoolwork a little more seriously from now on, too," added Poppy's mom. "You're not a baby anymore."

"Well, if I'm not a baby, can I walk to school by myself, instead of walking with Astrid?" asked Poppy. "And can I go into town alone on the bus?"

"Definitely not!" said her mother quickly. "You're far too young for that."

Poppy sighed and ate her breakfast, ignoring Astrid's smirks. This conversation had summed up *exactly* what was bad about being a tweenager. Everyone told you that you were still too young to do fun stuff. But at the same time, they expected you to do a whole lot of extra chores because you were no longer a little kid! It was totally unfair.

*But*, Poppy thought, giving her long ponytail a little pat, *if I wasn't a tweenager, then I wouldn't be a tweenie genie, either!*

Imagine if her parents knew that she'd spent the previous night learning about granting wishes and zooming around on a magic carpet! Just thinking about it gave Poppy a shiver of excitement. And it made her more determined than ever to get her bottle back from Astrid.

After breakfast, Astrid and Poppy headed off to school together. Usually Astrid walked a few feet ahead, as though it were embarrassing to walk with her little sister. She always tried to make Poppy carry her bag for her, too. "You should see it as an honor," she would say. Poppy always refused, of course.

But this morning, everything was the opposite. Astrid wouldn't leave Poppy's side.

And there was no way she was letting Poppy hold her bag while the genie bottle was inside!

When they were around the block, Astrid turned grumpily to Poppy.

"What's going on, Poppy?" she demanded. "Mom told me to stack the dirty dishes after breakfast and believe me, famous people do not stack dishes. Plus we've passed loads of people already, but no one has asked for my autograph. I'm starting to think your wish didn't work. So, here's a warning: If it hasn't worked by the time we reach school, guess what I'll be talking about in Show and Tell this morning?" Astrid patted her schoolbag and gave Poppy a menacing look.

"Astrid, we're in middle school," Poppy pointed out, trying to look calm. "We don't do Show and Tell anymore."

110

"Maybe not usually," said Astrid darkly, "but I suspect they would make an exception when they see what I've got."

Poppy didn't say anything, but she knew Astrid was right. Everyone would be *very* interested to hear they had a genie at school. It was only a matter of time before Astrid realized that the wish hadn't worked, and Poppy would be no closer to getting her bottle back.

All too soon, they arrived at their school and nothing had happened.

"Right," said Astrid loudly, as they stepped onto the school grounds. "I'm officially sick of waiting for this wish to kick in. Unless something happens *right now* I'm going to . . ."

And then something did happen. Something totally unexpected and really quite remarkable. It started off as nothing more than

a faint humming noise. And then steadily, the noise began to get louder and louder.

Poppy and Astrid stood perfectly still, listening. What was going on?

# Chapter 8

Finally, the noise grew so loud and came so close that Poppy realized what it was. It was hundreds of schoolkids, all chanting one word.

"Astrid! Astrid! ASTRID!"

Astrid's face lit up. "The wish is working!" she exclaimed.

"Is it?" said Poppy doubtfully. She hadn't thought for a moment that the wish would *really* work. How could it, after all, if her wish routine wasn't right?

*There must be some other explanation*, she told herself. But what that was exactly, she wasn't sure.

A moment later, Astrid was completely surrounded by hundreds of excited kids calling her name, with expressions of crazed devotion on their faces. They pushed and jostled each other, trying to get closer to Astrid.

"Astrid!" they called. "Can I have your autograph? Can I sit next to you at lunchtime? Can I have my picture taken with you?"

Astrid didn't seem at all alarmed by the crowd. Far from it! She jumped up onto a bench and waved, grinning broadly. She even blew kisses. In fact, she acted like she'd been famous her entire life. The crowd grew by the second and Poppy found herself being pushed further and further away from Astrid and

from the bag in which her bottle was stashed.

"Who is the most fabulous, fantastic, and FAMOUS person in the entire world?" Astrid shouted over the noise.

"YOU ARE!" the crowd thundered back.

Astrid looked triumphant.

*If only I were up in front right now, while she's showing off in front of the crowd,* thought Poppy longingly. But there was no way she could push through the throng to get anywhere near Astrid now.

A moment later, the crowd picked Astrid up and she was carried away. Cameras flashed as she went and cheers filled the air every time Astrid so much as opened her mouth.

Poppy followed behind, feeling very puzzled. What was going on? Was it possible that Astrid actually *had* become famous?

It was then that Poppy noticed something very unusual. The kids who were still arriving at school for the day didn't seem at all excited to see Astrid. In fact, they looked totally confused by all the fuss. But the moment they stepped onto the school grounds, a look of devotion swept over their faces and they rushed to join the mob of Astrid-lovers.

*Astrid IS super-famous, but only at school,* realized Poppy, chuckling. *My wish routine is only half worked out, so it only half granted Astrid's wish.* She felt a little surge of pride at having granted her first wish, even if it wasn't totally perfect.

Just then, one of Astrid's fans pushed past, knocking Poppy's backpack off her shoulder. The genie jotter fell out and opened to the page on which the Golden Laws were written.

The writing seemed to have grown even bigger!

★ Golden Law # 1:
Do NOT reveal your identity
to ANYONE.

★ Golden Law # 2:
Tweenies are NOT ALLOWED to
grant wishes until they have passed
their first examination.

All the pride Poppy had felt in granting Astrid's wish quickly vanished.

*I've been a tweenie genie for less than one day and I've already broken both of those laws,* she thought, biting her lip. She knew Lexie wouldn't be impressed if she found out.

"Isn't this just crazy?" said a familiar voice behind her. It was Claudette. Behind her stood the Clothes Club girls.

"Look at the way all these people are acting," sniffed Claudette. "It's embarrassing."

Poppy found herself smiling. It was such a relief to find someone, *anyone* who wasn't besotted by Astrid.

"It is insane, isn't it?" she agreed.

"A style-icon like Astrid should be treated with more respect," said Claudette disapprovingly.

Poppy stared at Claudette in dismay. "Excuse me?" she said, hoping she'd heard incorrectly. But then she noticed Claudette's T-shirt. On the front was a picture of Astrid. On the back was written "I ♥ Astrid!"

"Astrid is the kind of person we need on the front cover of *School Style* magazine," Claudette declared, pulling out her camera.

"The entire next edition of *School Style* will be devoted to her. And the one after that, too."

"Well, that will make a pleasant change," muttered Poppy to herself. Every other edition of *School Style* had featured only one person—Claudette!

"Can you believe that Astrid is your sister?" added Claudette, sighing enviously. "You are so, so lucky."

Poppy walked off. She couldn't stand much more of this! She even wanted the bell to ring, so that class could start and things could get back to normal. But at nine o'clock, when the bell was supposed to ring, a message came on over the school loudspeaker from Principal Smith.

"In honor of our incredibly famous student, we are declaring today Astrid Day!

Normal classes are cancelled. Instead, please come to the multipurpose hall for an all-day tribute assembly in Astrid's honor."

Poppy groaned and shook her head in dismay. The wish might only work at school. But it was working way too well! Everyone in the whole place had gone completely crazy. Everywhere Poppy looked, she saw students wearing "I ♥ Astrid" T-shirts and "Astrid is Awesome" wristbands. The school choir had gathered in the courtyard and was singing songs about Astrid. The basketball team had started calling itself the Astrid Avengers and the arty kids were painting an enormous portrait of Astrid on the outside of the hall. It was at least nine feet tall!

*Is there one sane person left around here?* wondered Poppy. Then she turned a corner

and bumped into her teacher, Ms. Kelly.

"Poppy, I'm glad to see you," Ms. Kelly exclaimed. She had something rolled up under her arm.

"Hi, Ms. Kelly," said Poppy, relieved. If anyone would be unaffected by the wish, it would be Ms. Kelly. She was a very sensible person and not at all the sort to go gaga over someone famous—especially not Astrid!

"I have a job for you," said Ms. Kelly. "Can you help me put this sign up, please?"

Ms. Kelly undid the scroll and Poppy's heart fell to her toes when she saw what it said.

## ASTRID MILLER MIDDLE SCHOOL

"We've renamed the school in honor of your sister!" Ms. Kelly explained excitedly. "This sign is going across the old school sign

out in front. What do you think?"

"I'll tell you what I think," said Poppy furiously. "I think it's the most stup—"

But Poppy was interrupted by the sound of cheering. Ms. Kelly let out a high-pitched squeal.

"Astrid must be coming!" she said, jumping up and down. "I just *have* to get her autograph! See you at the tribute assembly, Poppy." Then she ran off.

There was absolutely no way that Poppy was going to an all-day Astrid tribute assembly. Even a five-minute tribute would have been too long. But she knew that this might be her big chance to get her bottle back. So while everyone else was hurrying into the hall, Poppy hid behind a tree. Once everyone was inside, she sneaked up and watched through a window.

Astrid was up on the stage, sitting on the special chair that was usually reserved for the principal. Beside her was an enormous screen. Everyone else was sitting in front of her, totally spellbound. Astrid-mania was showing no signs of lessening. In fact, the crowd seemed even more captivated than before. Everytime Astrid did anything—*anything at all*—the crowd went wild. When she waved, they cheered. If she smiled, they screamed. When she tried to speak, they roared with excitement at the tops of their voices. At one point, Astrid sneezed and several students (plus two teachers) fainted!

*Right,* decided Poppy. *Time to put a stop to this!*

It was then that she spotted Astrid's schoolbag, sitting next to her on the stage.

*I just need to get my genie bottle out of there,* thought Poppy, looking at the bag. *There must be a way!*

Principal Smith took the stage, beaming joyfully. "I have such a treat for you all!" she announced. "We have put together a film about Astrid's time at our humble school. Sadly, it's only four hours long. But once it's finished, we can watch it over again." Then she dimmed the lights and shut the curtains.

Outside the hall, Poppy's heart leapt with excitement.

*This is my chance!* she realized. The room was dark now, and everyone would be so caught up with the Astrid film that they wouldn't notice Poppy sneaking in and grabbing something out of Astrid's bag.

Stealthily, Poppy sneaked around to the

door at the back of the hall. The door creaked slightly as she opened it. Poppy froze, but no one turned around. They were all far too engrossed in the film. Poppy could dimly make out Astrid, sitting up next to the screen, craning her head so she could watch the film, too.

Poppy padded quietly up to the front of the hall, hiding herself in the shadows. When she got to the front just below the stage, she paused. This was the tricky bit. To grab Astrid's bag, she would have to leave the safety of the shadows, and sneak across to where Astrid was sitting. It would only work if no one happened to look away from the screen. Poppy scanned the audience. Everyone was transfixed by the Astrid film.

*OK*, thought Poppy bravely. *Here goes!*

With a pounding heart, Poppy crept across the room until she was right next to Astrid's

bag. Then she reached out and felt her fingers close around the smooth glass of the bottle.

*I've got it!* she thought excitedly. But just as she was about to slide the bag towards her, it was yanked out of her grasp. Then, before she knew what was happening, someone had grabbed her arm and pulled her outside.

# Chapter 9

It was, of course, Astrid who had pulled Poppy outside.

"If you think I'm going to let you steal back that genie bottle, you can think again," Astrid snapped, pushing her bag firmly onto her shoulder. "Especially now I'm ready to make my next wish."

Poppy looked at her sister nervously. She hated to think what Astrid would wish for now!

"Maybe you should wait a bit before making your next wish, Astrid?" she suggested.

But Astrid shook her head. "I'm not waiting," she insisted. "I'm totally sick of all these people following me around. I can't even go to the bathroom without them trailing along! I'm sick of them taking pictures of me all the time—especially as they won't get rid of the bad ones. But most of all I'm sick of them not actually listening to me!"

"Really?" said Poppy, pretending to look surprised. "They don't listen to *you*?"

Astrid shook her head gloomily. "I know. It's unbelievable. I thought they'd all be fascinated to hear my thoughts and stuff. But whenever I try to talk they just cheer right over the top of me. It's so annoying. You know what I wish? I wish that no one knew who I

128

was anymore."

"Wish granted!" Poppy grinned, promptly starting her wish routine before Astrid could change her mind. This time Poppy ended it by twinkling her fingers. It felt like a pretty good move, but there was no puff of smoke.

"I hereby grant Astrid's wish," she said dramatically. "No one will know who she is anymore!"

Poppy tried to act like she was sure this wish was going to work. But inside she felt very jittery. The last wish seemed to have worked, but it might also have been a total fluke!

"I don't feel any different," said Astrid flatly. "It hasn't worked."

"Look!" said Poppy. "Everyone is coming out of the assembly."

Sure enough, the crowd had started filing

out of the hall, looking as though they weren't at all sure why they'd been in there in the first place. And they walked right by Astrid without paying her the slightest bit of attention.

One girl had an "I ♥ Astrid!" banner in her hand. She turned to a boy and said, "Do you know why I'm carrying this banner?"

"No," replied the boy. "And I have no idea why I'm wearing this T-shirt either. Who is Astrid, anyway?"

Astrid beamed. "I'm not famous anymore!" she said delightedly.

Then Ms. Kelly walked past. She stopped beside Poppy and Astrid.

"Hurry to class please, Poppy," she said. "We have wasted a lot of time today on an assembly for someone that no one seems to know." Then

she looked at Astrid. "Are you ⸮

should report to the front office."

Astrid winked at Poppy. "Ms. Kelly, it's me, Astrid," she said. "I was in your class last year, remember?"

"You certainly were not!" responded Ms. Kelly indignantly. "I've never seen you before."

"Astrid is in Miss Kennedy's class," said Poppy, grabbing Astrid by the arm. "I'll take her there."

Astrid didn't seem at all bothered by suddenly being completely unknown. "This is going to be so fun!" she giggled. "It's almost like being invisible. If Miss Kennedy can't remember who I am, then I guess she'll forget that I'm supposed to be on hall duty today."

It definitely looked like this next wish had worked. But Poppy suspected that it probably vasn't perfect, either. *I wonder if this wish only works at school, like the last one?*

She soon had a chance to find out. Astrid's friend, Nicole, had just been dropped off out in front of school. She saw Astrid and waved.

"Hey, Astrid!" Nicole called. "I had to go to the dentist this morning. Have I missed much?"

Astrid laughed. "Wait till I tell you!"

But as Nicole stepped in through the school gates, she frowned and shook her head. Then she looked around, slightly dazed. "Hi, Poppy," she said. "Who's your friend? Is she new?"

"Nic, it's *me*!" giggled Astrid.

Nicole shrugged. "Sorry, I don't know who you are," she replied politely.

"But we've been best friends since first grade!" said Astrid, looking a little anxious all of a sudden.

132

"No," said Nicole, walking off briskly. "I've never met you."

Astrid went very pale. It was like she'd only just realized exactly what she'd wished for. "I've got to go," she muttered, hurrying off after Nicole.

*Well,* thought Poppy, watching her go. *Lexie was right about normies. They make terrible wishes!*

Astrid's second wish made things at school go back to normal—for Poppy at least. It felt like any other ordinary school day, except that she had lots more things than usual to think about.

She sneaked her *Genie Culture and History* book onto her lap during class so that she could study it when Ms. Kelly wasn't watching. But even

133

when she got a moment to read a few lines, the words seemed to make no sense. At the end of an hour, she'd barely finished a page. And she couldn't remember what it had been about!

## DID YOU KNOW?

The textbook that Poppy is reading is a backward speed-reader. If read the normie way, from left to right, the words simply refuse to stick in the memory. This is so that if a normie ever comes across it, they won't remember a word it says. But when read upside down, back to front by a genie, the words suddenly make perfect sense!

*I may as well read it backward*! thought Poppy crossly. She flipped the book upside down and the words suddenly made a lot more sense. Even better, the book suddenly seemed a lot quicker to read. Half an hour into her English class, Poppy had finished reading three thick chapters.

*I'm not sure what's going on here,* thought Poppy happily, *but I wish all my textbooks were like this.*

When the bell rang at the end of the day, Astrid was waiting for Poppy in front of her classroom, looking really annoyed.

"This wish has turned out even worse than the last one," she complained. "It doesn't matter how many times I tell people who I am, a minute later, they've forgotten again. I had to enroll as a new student fifty times today!"

"So, are you ready to make your third wish?" asked Poppy hopefully. Once Astrid

had made her third wish, she would have to return the bottle.

"Yes," snapped Astrid. "I wish that I'd never found that stupid bottle in the first place!"

Poppy nodded, trying not to grin. She couldn't have come up with a better wish herself. But would she be able to grant it? She wanted it to work properly this time. Properly and completely.

"OK, I'll grant your final wish," Poppy said.

*Twist, snake hands, side step.* Poppy paused. What *was* that missing move? It had to be something really obvious. Something she'd done a thousand times before ...

There was one move she hadn't tried. But surely it was just way too ridiculous! Then again, it couldn't hurt to try. Cautiously, Poppy touched her nose with her tongue.

The effect was instantaneous. *Whoomph!* A cloud of silvery smoke puffed up around her feet. Poppy nearly burst out laughing. She'd finally found it! The missing move.

Astrid raised an eyebrow suspiciously. "What are you up to?" she said. But even as she spoke, a vague expression came over Astrid's face.

Then a moment later, she grinned at Poppy in her old, familiar, annoying way. "Hi Poppy," she said, like she'd just seen her. "Did you find out what your special talent was today? Don't tell me you don't have one, because no one could be *that* ordinary!"

Poppy rolled her eyes, pretending to look annoyed. But secretly, she was overjoyed. The final wish had worked! Now there was just one more thing to do.

"Hey Astrid, let me carry your bag home for you," Poppy said sugary sweetly. "It would be my *honor*."

"Sure thing!" said Astrid, swinging the bag right into Poppy's arms.

The bag was really heavy, but Poppy didn't mind. The instant Astrid's back was turned, Poppy quietly unzipped the bag, took out her genie bottle and safely stashed it away in her own backpack.

# Chapter 10

Jake, Hazel, and Rose were already at the Training Center Bottle when Poppy arrived that evening.

Jake gave her a puzzled look. "What happened to you this morning?" he asked. "You left in a huge hurry. And you looked pretty green."

Poppy shrugged. "I was just ready to get back home," she said. She was pretty sure she could trust Jake now, but she didn't really want to talk about her wish-granting adventures.

"Ready for your exam, tweenies?" asked Lexie. "It's tomorrow night, don't forget!"

"Yes, Lexie!" chorused the tweenies.

"Let's do some studying then," said Lexie. "Hopefully, you all figured out the correct way to read your genie textbooks."

Poppy was glad to see the others all nodding. She didn't want anyone to fail the exam.

"Who can tell me why genies live in bottles?" asked Lexie.

Jake's hand shot up. "Originally, genies lived in bottles because the normies used to catch us and keep us in them," he said. "But now genies choose to live in bottles because they are a good way of disguising where we live. We can live in normie houses without them even knowing we're there."

Lexie nodded in approval. "Good. OK, who can tell me three ways to spot a genie in the normie world?"

Hazel put her hand up. "They are always wearing at least one bangle," she said. "And they are usually wearing one really bright piece of clothing—even if it's just a sock—because genies love bright things."

"Going well," said Lexie. "And one more?"

Hazel thought for a moment. "Oh, yeah," she giggled. "Genies never eat sandwich crusts. And I totally understand why. Yuck!"

"Very good," said Lexie. "Who can tell me when we're supposed to say *your wish is my command*?"

"Trick question!" responded Rose quickly. "We *never* say that, not anymore. Genies said

that ages ago, back when we still called normies "master" and "mistress," but we definitely don't say it these days. It would just make the normie think they were the boss of us."

"And aren't they the boss of us?" asked Lexie, pretending to look surprised.

"No way!" chorused all the tweenies together. "We're the boss of ourselves."

Lexie laughed, and then she looked at Poppy. "One for you now," she said. "Can you tell me the genie wish-granting motto?"

Poppy thought hard. She remembered reading this motto. What was it again?

"*No swerving if the normie is deserving*," she blurted out.

"What do you think that means, Poppy?" asked Lexie.

"Um," said Poppy slowly, "I guess it means

that if the normie really deserves to have their wish granted, then genies shouldn't try to get out of it."

Lexie smiled. "Yes, exactly," she said. "We genies have a reputation for being a bit tricky. This might be true, but genies are also able to recognize a good wish, or an important wish, if we come across it."

Then Lexie looked around. "Time for something a bit more uplifting now," she said. "Levitation!"

A ripple of excitement ran through the class. Jake nudged Poppy and gave her a cheeky grin. "Race you to the ceiling!" he whispered.

"You're on!" Poppy whispered back confidently. Who knew—maybe levitation would turn out to be her special skill?

When the floor was clear, Lexie got everyone

to sit cross-legged on the floor, with their eyes shut and their hands on their knees.

"Now, the key to levitation is to think light, airy, cheerful thoughts," Lexie said. "Clouds are a good thing to focus on. So are hot-air balloons. In fact, all balloons are good, except popped ones."

Poppy tried to picture a kite, flying high in the air. But for some annoying reason, her imaginary kite kept getting tangled in an imaginary tree.

"The second step," continued Lexie, "is to imagine there's a piece of string attached to your head that's pulling you up toward the sky."

Poppy tried it, but she didn't feel like she was moving. It felt like there was a rope across her lap, tying her down.

*Maybe I've moved and I just haven't noticed,*

she wondered, opening one eye to check.

No. She was definitely still on the ground. But the rest of the class—including Lexie—had disappeared! Then Poppy looked up. Lexie and the other tweenies were all floating, cross-legged, near the top of the Training Center Bottle!

Poppy felt a wave of frustration pass over her. Why did she find all the genie stuff so hard?

"Try wiggling your nose," Lexie called down to her. "Sometimes that helps."

So Poppy tried wiggling her nose. Then she wiggled her mouth, her tongue, her toes, even her ears! But nothing helped.

"I'm never going to get this!" she said in frustration.

"OK, back down to the ground, everyone," commanded Lexie.

146

Poppy watched enviously as the other three tweenies descended, laughing and joking with each other. They made it look so easy. Why couldn't *she* do it?

"Well done, tweenies. You can have the rest of the night off," said Lexie.

Everyone stared at her in surprise.

"It's up to you how you choose to spend this time," Lexie continued. "Go to the Emerald Mall if you like, and choose an outfit to wear to the Graduation Ball tomorrow night. Your outfits are a gift from the Genie Royal Family, so choose whatever you like. But don't spend all night there. You should spend at least a little time studying."

Then Lexie turned to Poppy. "Poppy," she said. "You stay here with me. We'll work on your levitation."

Poppy's heart sank. She didn't want to miss out on going to the Emerald Mall with the others!

"Um, Lexie?" said Jake. "I really think Poppy should come to the mall with me. You see, I only ever wear jeans or my football gear. If I don't get some help, I'm going to turn up to the ball in something shocking."

"Well, that's a risk we'll have to take," said Lexie drily. "Poppy has work to do."

Jake shrugged. "Fine," he said. "But if I end up wearing something dumb, it's not my fault!"

Once everyone was gone, Lexie went through levitating with Poppy again. But try as she might, Poppy just couldn't get off the ground. Not even an inch.

148

Lexie watched her silently. Poppy kept waiting for Lexie to tell her that she wasn't trying hard enough. But Lexie didn't say that. In fact, when she finally spoke, she said, "Get out your Location Lamp and let's go."

"Go where?" asked Poppy, astonished.

"You need something to wear to your graduation," declared Lexie. "And besides, you'd be amazed what a change of scenery can do when you're trying to work something out."

Lexie took Poppy back to Madame di Silver's shop. She greeted Lexie and Poppy warmly.

"Madame," said Lexie. "Poppy needs something to wear for the Graduation Ball tomorrow night. Something from the *Special Collection*, I think."

Madame looked at Lexie in astonishment. "Really?" she said. "The *Special Collection*?"

Lexie nodded. "Yes," she said.

Madame put her hand on the wall of the shop and a panel slid back, revealing a secret room. Lexie stepped through the opening, and Poppy followed.

The room was filled with clothes. But these weren't ordinary clothes. They were the most beautiful and unusual garments Poppy had ever seen. For instance, one top was decorated with birds. When Poppy touched the material, the birds stretched open their wings and began to sing. Hanging next to the top was a pair of genie pants, dotted with tightly closed flower buds. But when Poppy came close, the flowers burst into bloom. Poppy could see why these clothes were part of a Special Collection.

"What about this?" suggested Madame, handing Poppy an outfit made out of material the color of the ocean. It had tiny starfish and shells embroidered across it, and as Poppy watched, a school of sapphire-colored fish flashed across the surface and then disappeared from view.

"Do you like it?" asked Madame.

"It's incredible," gulped Poppy.

"Well, try it on then!" urged Madame, smiling.

Poppy didn't need any further encouragement. And the outfit was a perfect fit!

"It's like it was *made* for you!" exclaimed Madame. "Which is funny, because of course it was actually made for ... "

But then a strange thing happened. Poppy saw Lexie frown and shake her head slightly

material the color of the ocean →

tiny starfish and shells

sapphire-colored fish

Collection outfit

at Madame, and Madame stopped midway through her sentence.

"Why don't you try levitating again, Poppy?" said Lexie, smiling brightly as if nothing weird had just happened. "Let's see if the new clothes make a difference."

Poppy nodded. These special new clothes *did* somehow make her feel light and floaty. She sat down with her eyes closed, and tried to let the levitation just happen by itself. A second passed. Poppy could feel Lexie and Madame holding their breaths. Another second passed. Then another. And still Poppy was no closer to rising off the floor.

Then Poppy did something that she never, *ever* did. She burst into tears!

"It's hopeless!" she cried. "I'm never going to get this!"

Madame quickly fetched her a cup of tea (which was the color of roses, but smelled like chocolate). Lexie came and sat down beside her while she drank it.

"Have you worked out your wish routine?" she asked quietly.

Poppy wiped her nose and nodded.

"Well then, there's no reason to think you won't work this out, too," said Lexie in a surprisingly kind voice.

"But maybe I'm not cut out to be a genie,"

Poppy burst out. She hadn't meant to say it, but the words had come out from deep within her.

But Lexie shook her head. "No, that's not the problem here," she said softly. "You'll probably be surprised to hear this, but I believe you could be a great genie one day—maybe even one of the best. You remind me a lot of Princess Alexandria."

Poppy looked up and wiped her nose. "Do you know the Princess?" she asked, impressed.

"Well, sort of," replied Lexie, looking a little embarrassed. "What I know about her is that she had a lot of trouble when she was in tweenie training. But it wasn't because she lacked talent. She just needed to learn how to control it. I have a feeling you're the same."

It was nice to hear Lexie say these things, but Poppy didn't really think they could be true. "If

I'm so talented, why can't I levitate?" she asked.

"Well, I can think of a reason," said Lexie, looking carefully at Poppy. "Sometimes, genies can't levitate if there is something weighing them down. Like a secret. Or because they feel guilty about a rule they've broken."

Poppy felt sick. She'd broken loads of rules by granting Astrid's three wishes. And she hadn't told anyone about it, so it was definitely a secret. Was that stopping her from levitating?

"The Graduation Ball is tomorrow night," said Lexie seriously. "You need to work out what's weighing you down by then."

Poppy bit her lip. "And if I don't work it out?" she asked nervously.

Lexie sighed. "Then I'm afraid you won't pass."

# Chapter 11

The next day at school was hard for Poppy. She still had a few chapters of her *Genie Culture and History* textbook to read. This shouldn't have taken long, but she found it hard to concentrate. Her thoughts kept whirling around about what she should do.

*If I don't own up to breaking the Golden Rules, then I'm never going to rise off the ground,* she thought. *But if I DO tell someone, I might not be allowed to graduate!*

It seemed like a problem with no solution.

When Poppy finally got home from school, she told her mom she had a terrible headache (which was true) and escaped to her room.

Poppy quickly squeezed inside her genie bottle, which had been safely hidden inside a pillowcase, and then flopped with relief onto her bed.

*I need to relax before I do anything else*, she decided, adjusting the dial above her bed so that it clicked into Rainforest Mode. Instantly, the image of a thick, cool rainforest was projected onto the walls of her bottle. The sound of birdsong filled the air and Poppy's bed was transformed into a pile of soft green ferns and mosses. Poppy's headache

disappeared and she found herself drifting off to sleep.

After about fifteen minutes, Poppy opened her eyes. She knew she hadn't slept long, but her mind felt much clearer.

*When I get to the ball, I'll tell Lexie about granting the wishes,* she decided. *And then I'll do such a good job in my exams that they HAVE to let me stay!*

Poppy jumped up and put on her Special Collection outfit. Even though what she'd decided to do was pretty scary, she felt good. She looked sternly at her reflection in the mirror.

"Next time I see YOU," she told herself, "I will be a Stage Two tweenie. Just you wait and see!"

It was the night of the ball. Poppy expected the Royal Palace Bottle to be grand. But she hadn't realized it would be *quite* so magnificent! All she could do was gaze around in utter astonishment. The palace was made entirely out of pink crystal, and the floor was inlaid with precious stones, set into gold. Flowing velvet curtains, the color of fire, hung around all the doorways, and chandeliers were suspended from the ceilings, their lights twinkling and glittering like a galaxy of stars.

Poppy suddenly felt shy. *Maybe I should just sneak back to my bottle before anyone sees me*, she thought. But she was too late. A grand-looking genie-butler stepped up to her and bowed very low.

"Welcome to the Royal Palace, Tweenie Poppy," he said. "Please follow me to the exam

area." He then led her to a room filled with four very comfortable-looking cushions. Beside them were four magic carpets, with food and drink resting on top. Music played softly in the background.

"It doesn't look like any exam room I've ever seen," said Poppy in surprise.

The butler chuckled. "We genies hate exams," he explained, "so we try to make them as pleasant as possible."

He handed Poppy a pair of slippers. They were made out of purple felt and were as soft as a baby rabbit. "Wear these during the exam," he said kindly. "They can tell when you're getting tense and will give your toes a rub."

Poppy put the slippers on. They were certainly very comfortable. She felt less nervous already!

Rose and Hazel bounded over, also wearing the slippers.

"Wow, you look amazing!" said Rose, staring at Poppy's dress in awe.

"So do you guys!" said Poppy. It was true. Both girls were dressed in very elegant genie pants and sparkly tops. Rose had decorated her high ponytail with a sequin headband, and Hazel was wearing a belt made of tiny silver bells.

"What about *my* outfit?" said another voice.

Poppy turned, and burst out laughing. It was Jake, wearing bright yellow silky pants and a matching shirt. On his head was a green, spiky turban.

"Jake," said Poppy, "I hate to tell you this, but you look like a pineapple."

Jake groaned. "I knew I'd mess it up!" he said. "I warned you I was hopeless at picking clothes."

"Just be careful you don't fall into the fruit salad!" giggled Rose.

"Luckily, we're not being tested on outfits," grinned Jake. "Tonight is about knowing your genie stuff backward and forward. Are you guys ready?"

"Yep!" replied Rose and Hazel together.

"Of course," said Poppy, although she was actually starting to feel very nervous. She wasn't at all sure she remembered anything from her *Genie Culture and History* book. And as for levitating—well, she had yet to actually get off the ground!

The butler rang a bell and said, "Tweenies, your written exam is about to begin. Please take a seat. An exam paper will appear before you shortly."

Instantly, Poppy felt her stomach do a flip of nervousness. This was it! She went and sat on one of the cushions. Right away, one of the magic carpets flew over, offering her a drink and tickling her arm with its tassels.

"Hey," whispered Jake. "Isn't that the annoying bath mat from the Emerald Mall?"

Right away, the carpet whacked him on the nose with one corner.

"Ouch!" said Jake, pulling back. "I was right!"

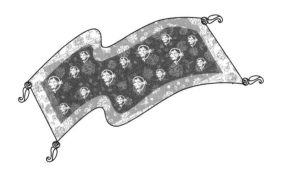

Poppy laughed and gave the carpet a pat. "Just ignore Jake," she whispered to it.

Just then, a sheet of paper and a pen appeared in front of each of the tweenies.

"You have exactly one genie hour to complete the exam," said the butler. "When the time is up, the paper will disappear. Good luck, tweenies!"

With a pounding heart, Poppy picked up her pen and looked at the first question:

*What is the genie wish-granting motto and what does it mean?*

For one horrible moment, Poppy's mind went blank. Around her, the others were scribbling away furiously. But then her slippers gave her toes a reassuring squeeze. It was just what Poppy needed right then.

*You know this*, she told herself sternly. *Just*

*put your head down and get on with it*. And then the motto popped into her head. *No swerving if the normie is deserving*.

Poppy picked up her pen and started to write.

"Time's up!" called the butler, just as Poppy filled in the last answer. She put down her pen and the exam paper disappeared in a flurry of stars. There was no changing anything now!

"Now, please follow me into the Royal Ballroom," said the butler. "It's time for the second part of your exam. You will be presented to the Genie Royal Family and demonstrate what you have learned in front of Princess Alexandria."

The tweenies all looked at each other and

followed the butler. There was a mixture of excitement and nervousness on each of their faces.

In the middle of the ballroom was a dance floor that gleamed like an enormous diamond— glittering and smooth. High above hung a vast chandelier made from multicolored precious stones that sent little rainbows around the room. The room was full of guests, all splendidly dressed. It seemed that all the dignitaries of the Genie Realm had come along that night.

As Poppy looked around, she saw that there was one person missing. Where was Lexie?

*She must be running late*, thought Poppy, puzzled. *Surely, she wouldn't miss the exam?*

Jake came over. "I don't know about you, but exams make me hungry," he whispered. "Let's get something to eat and drink before part two starts."

He waved his hand and a carpet swiftly approached, laden with snacks. Poppy stifled a giggle as it got close. It was the same carpet from before. But Jake hadn't recognized it yet. But when he tried to take something off the top, the carpet zipped sideways, so all Jake got was a handful of air.

"Not you again!" he groaned. "Get away from me, you big washcloth!"

"I don't know why you two can't get along," giggled Poppy, taking two of the purpliest, fizziest drinks she had ever seen from the top of the rug.

Then Madame di Silver glided over. "You look wonderful, Poppy!" she said.

"Thanks for choosing this outfit for me," said Poppy gratefully. "I never could have done it on my own. Everything in your shop is so beautiful."

"Oh, that outfit wasn't in my shop," replied Madame. "That's why it's so special. It was in Princess Alexandria's private collection. I've never seen her permit a tweenie to wear her things before. You should feel very honored."

Poppy frowned. "But it was *Lexie* who said

I could wear this outfit," she said, confused.

"Yes, that's right," said Madame di Silver, nodding. "The princess herself."

Poppy's mouth dropped open, but before she could say anything, a loud fanfare filled the room.

"Please stand for the entrance of the Genie Royal Family," proclaimed the butler.

An enormous puff of twinkling, golden smoke appeared in the middle of the dance floor, and a very elegant genie couple walked through the haze, arm in arm. They were dressed in purple, and each wore a gold crown on their heads. Poppy knew this was the Genie King and Queen.

This was followed by another puff of smoke—purple this time—and another genie appeared.

"Princess Alexandria!" announced the butler.

The princess stepped forward, dressed in

clothes that seemed to be made out of pure sunlight itself. On her head, she wore a tiny gold crown through which her long, black ponytail cascaded. But the most incredible thing of all about the princess was that she looked exactly like Lexie!

Poppy stood still, waiting for someone to say, "Hey, that's not Princess Alexandria!" But no one did. And when Lexie stepped out of the smoke, everyone bowed low.

"Let the Graduation Ball begin!" declared the princess, raising her hands up high and releasing streams of tiny stars into the room. Then she looked at the tweenies. "Good luck, you guys!" she said, and she winked at them in a *most* un-princess-like way.

# Chapter 12

The first tweenie to be called up was Hazel. She was introduced to the Royal Family, and then went through her wish routine, which she did perfectly. Her levitation was a little slow to start. But when she finally got off the ground, everyone clapped.

"Well done, Hazel," said Lexie warmly. "Now, let's check your results."

She lifted up an ancient-looking book with marbled pages and a leather cover. "This is the Tweenie Genie Yearbook," Lexie explained. "If you have passed both parts of your exam, your name will appear in it."

Lexie held up the opened book. Faintly at first, but with growing strength, letters appeared to spell out Hazel's name! The ballroom burst into delighted cheers.

Rose went next, and sailed through everything easily. Then it was Jake's turn. Poppy saw his face go white. As he walked passed, Poppy gave his arm a friendly squeeze.

"Good luck, pineapple-head!" she whispered.

Jake grinned, suddenly looking a whole lot less nervous. Poppy held her breath when Jake wobbled during his wish routine, and clapped with relief when the smoke puff appeared when he finished. As for his levitation—well, there was nothing to worry about there. It was perfect.

"Nice one!" Poppy breathed when his name appeared in the yearbook. So far no one had failed!

And then Poppy's name was called. But Poppy found herself frozen to the spot.

Jake nudged Poppy. "Go on, Teeny Weeny!" he muttered. "Get out there and wow them."

So, with her stomach fluttering like a bag of butterflies, Poppy walked out onto the dance floor.

"So, what do you want to start with?" asked Lexie. "Wish routine or levitation?"

"Wish routine," replied Poppy quickly. She knew she'd have to face the levitation eventually. But the longer she could put it off, the better!

Lexie nodded. "Fine," she said.

*Snake hands, double spin, slide, touch nose*

*with tongue*. Poppy had done the routine so many times now that it just felt completely natural. Everyone laughed when she did that final, silly move. But it was a friendly laugh, and they all cheered when the smoke puff of silver smoke billowed up around her.

But then came the moment Poppy had been dreading. The thing she couldn't put off any longer.

"Levitation," said Lexie firmly. "Are you ready?"

Poppy nodded, and sat down cross-legged on the dance floor. The purple fizzy drink gurgled in her stomach and Poppy felt sick. Now that the time had come, she wasn't so sure she was brave enough to tell Lexie about her big secret after all. Especially not in front of all these people!

*But I have to,* she told herself, *or I'm never*

*going to get off the ground*. And that would mean she'd never graduate to Stage Two tweenie genie training. It meant other things, too. She'd have to give up her lovely genie bottle. She'd never get another chance to fly on a magic carpet. And she'd probably never see Rose or Hazel or Jake again. Once she thought of it like that, her decision didn't seem so hard to make after all.

"Lexie," Poppy said. "I have something to tell you." Then she took a deep breath and closed her eyes. It would be much easier to tell Lexie what had happened if she couldn't see her!

She began to talk. She explained all about how Astrid had found her bottle and about how she got stuck in the normie world, unable to get her bottle back. And she explained all about the wishes, and how they had half worked, even before she had her wish routine worked out. The whole room was silent as she spoke. Then, when she'd finally finished, Poppy opened her eyes.

What she saw surprised her. Or, more precisely, she was surprised by what she didn't see. Where was everyone? For that matter, where was the floor? Poppy looked down. The floor was far below her, and all the guests were down there, staring up at her. Then Poppy felt something tickling the top of her head. It was the chandelier!

"How did I get up here?" asked Poppy, perplexed.

"You levitated, of course!" called Lexie. "But you'd better come back down now."

"OK, I'll try," said Poppy. She tried to think of some heavy things, and the first thing that popped into her head was an elephant sitting

177

on a bus. It was a strange thing to think of, but it worked and Poppy started sinking.

As Poppy's feet touched the floor, the room erupted into cheers. She had done her wish routine correctly. She'd even levitated! And the written exam had felt pretty easy.

*Is it possible that I've actually passed?* Poppy wondered excitedly.

The crowd clearly thought she had! Poppy's eyes turned hopefully to the yearbook. But her name wasn't there.

"Oh," she said, a lump rising in her throat. "I failed."

"What makes you think that?" asked Lexie softly.

"Because my name isn't in the yearbook," Poppy replied miserably.

Lexie smiled at her. "You are so determined

to believe you are ordinary, aren't you, Poppy?" she said. "Your name does appear in the yearbook. Just not in this part."

Lexie opened the book to another page. At the top of the page was the heading, Golden Genies.

"With every group of tweenies," Lexie explained, "there is usually one who shows such promise that she is considered Golden. And you, Poppy, are one of them."

Sure enough, Poppy's name was there, right at the bottom of the page, written in sparkling gold letters.

"But, that's not possible!" said Poppy, shaking her head. "I can't be a Golden Genie. I made way too many mistakes. It took me much longer than the others to get my wish routine right. And I kept opening my genie jotter without using the key, remember?"

Lexie and the King and Queen burst out laughing. Poppy stared at them. Why wasn't she in trouble?

"We're still disappointed that you broke the rules. But we're laughing because the reasons you are giving us are the exact same ones we think prove that you are a good genie," explained Lexie. "Possibly a great one, if trained properly. The signs were there right

from the start. Remember how easily you got into your genie bottle the first time? Most tweenies really struggle with that. And as for opening the genie jotter without a key—well, usually only Stage Three tweenies are powerful enough to do that. And you're behaving like you broke it! And let's not forget that your wishes half worked, even though your wish routine wasn't complete."

Poppy could hardly believe her ears.

"But it was when I saw you fly that magic carpet around the Emerald Mall that I really knew you were extra special," Lexie continued. "I've never seen a Stage One tweenie get a carpet off the ground, let alone fly it."

"You saw me flying the carpet?" said Poppy nervously.

Lexie laughed at her anxious expression.

"Oh, yes," she said. "You were flying one of *my* carpets, after all. I always make sure that there are a couple of palace carpets patrolling the mall when I take tweenies there. You guys have a tendency to wander off, despite my warnings."

Poppy's face went hot. It was embarrassing to think that Lexie knew exactly what she'd been up to that day in the Emerald Mall. The magic carpet whooshed over, and pushed a drink towards her with one of its corners.

"I think that carpet has taken a liking to you," smiled Lexie.

Poppy gave it a pat. "I like it, too," she said.

"Consider it yours, then," said Lexie. "Golden Genies always receive a prize. I will have it sent to your normie home tomorrow. Congratulations, Poppy. You should be proud of yourself."

There were so many things that Poppy

wanted to say right then. But all she could manage was, "Thank you."

She'd passed. And she'd passed really well. It was a wonderful feeling.

When Poppy joined the other tweenies, Rose and Hazel hugged her so tightly she could hardly breathe. But Jake stood back. For a horrible moment, Poppy wondered if he might be a bit jealous. But then his face broke into its usual, cheeky smile.

"You might be a Golden Genie to everyone else," he grinned, "but to me you'll always be Teeny Weeny. So don't go getting a big head, OK?"

Poppy rolled her eyes. "Somehow, I don't think that'll be possible with you as a friend, pineapple-head!" she laughed.

## One More Thing

**W**ednesday, October 20th, 4pm

Remember way back in Chapter One when we talked about people who stand out? Those kinds of people who have a certain something special about them? Go back and re-read it if you like.

Well, it's not like Poppy turned into one of those people overnight. After all, a genie—especially a tweenie genie—is supposed to blend in. But at the same time, a few people *did* notice a change in Poppy on Wednesday. Ms. Kelly did. She couldn't place what it was about Poppy that had changed, so she put it down to growing up and becoming more responsible, because these are the kinds of things adults always think. And she decided to give Poppy more work to do, which is what adults also always think is the best thing in these circumstances.

A few kids noticed something different about Poppy, too. She suddenly had a certain something that made them turn and stare when she walked by. Something that made her seem, well, a touch out of the ordinary.

One of the people who noticed was Claudette. She came up to Poppy at lunchtime the day after the Genie Graduation Ball.

"Hey, Poppy," she said. "I was wondering

if you would like to be on the front cover of *School Style*?"

"I'm not having a makeover, Claudette," said Poppy firmly. "I'm quite happy with the way I look."

"You should be," said Claudette. "Your bangle and your high ponytail—they look great. I think you might be about to start a whole new trend! So how about it?"

Poppy laughed. "Well, maybe," she said. She was in too good a mood to say no, even to Claudette.

When Poppy rushed home from school that afternoon, there was a long cardboard box on the hallway table, covered in glittery stamps and addressed to her. Poppy tried sneaking it into her room, where she could open it in private. But Astrid caught her.

"What's that?" she asked curiously. "Another birthday present?"

"No, it's just something I won," said Poppy, blushing.

"You *won* something?" said Astrid incredulously. "Open it up. Let me see!"

So Poppy opened the box, and out fell the magic carpet. But it was behaving like it wasn't magic at all. It was keeping very still and limp.

"A scruffy-looking rug," said Astrid, sounding disappointed. "What a weird prize. You can't put that on the mantelpiece."

Poppy saw one of the tassels flick ever so slightly. "It's not scruffy, it's beautiful," she said, giving the carpet a reassuring pat. "And it's going on my bedroom floor, right where it belongs." Then she went to her room.

As she laid the carpet down, she noticed a gold-trimmed card pinned to the back.

Well done, Poppy! Take a day off. But please report back to the training center tomorrow night—Stage Two training is about to begin!

Lexie xD